CW01402201

200651300

SINS OF THE FLESH

BY THE SAME AUTHOR

SINS OF THE FLESH

Julian Fane

Book Guild Publishing
Sussex, England

First published in Great Britain in 2008 by
The Book Guild Ltd
Pavilion View
19 New Road
Brighton, BN1 1UF

Typesetting in Garamond by
Keyboard Services, Luton, Bedfordshire

Printed in Great Britain by
CPI Antony Rowe

A catalogue record for this book is available from
The British Library

ISBN 978 1 84624 223 6

CHAPTER ONE

A weekday morning in the eternal city. A Roman morning in the twenty-first century. The month October, the temperature warm, the sky the vivid colour reserved for the Mediterranean region. Noise, of course. Scene the roadway outside the Hotel Universal located in an alley bearing the grandiose name, *Vicolo Garibaldi.*

A minibus had drawn up by the hotel. A shirt-sleeved employee was wheeling and carrying a suitcase from the hotel to the bus – there was no uniformed commissionaire. The driver of the bus was helping him to stow the suitcase in a luggage compartment. Two people emerged from the hotel and stood together at the top of the steps to the road. They were obviously English, she wearing something tweedy and with a capacious bag slung over her shoulder, he in cavalry twill and a blazer with brass buttons. They talked, they smiled at each other, they embraced – a prolonged embrace without a noticeable kiss – and she descended the steps, smiled at the hotel porter, then at the driver who ushered her into the bus, which must have been picking up passengers on behalf of a particular airline. The diesel engine roared and the bus

1

moved away in the direction of the Leonardo da Vinci Airport. The woman waved at the man standing at the top of the steps, he waved back, but the bus was already on its way.

Every picture tells a story. The couple were not young, perhaps in their later forties. They looked healthy. He was taller than most Italian men, handsome in the English style, he had ample strong blond hair and blue eyes, and his figure retained a certain litheness despite its solidity; she was also fair-haired, and her face with its red cheeks gave an impression of fluffiness without being hairy. They gave out signals that they were a married couple: they seemed to be comfortable together, but was it too comfortable, were they not altogether at ease? Their embrace was not lover-like. He did not bother to accompany her down the steps. Was his wave goodbye not quite so prompt as hers? These unanswered questions strayed into the realm of suspicion. They had been on holiday in Rome, celebrating something, having a good time; on the other hand, one was staying put in the Hotel Universal and the other going elsewhere, home, or to rejoin a different man, or to return to work, or a duty of some description.

The sun shone on the person shielding his eyes from its rays as he watched the activities in the *Vicolo Garibaldi*. Busy people took short cuts through it. Amorous young girls strolled by with hands in the hip pockets of their boyfriends' jeans. A solitary girl in a see-through shirt and a minimal mini-skirt licking an ice-cream cornet passed by, a boy on a bicycle circled round her, she laughed at him, he laughed at her, and he pedalled on towards his destination.

The hotel porter emerged with a bucket and mop and apologised to the guest before he began to wash the steps; he called the guest Crisp, Signor Crisp.

The true story of the little drama recently enacted was that Emily Crisp was returning to England to look after her father, who had suffered another cardiac infarction, otherwise known as a heart attack. The Crisps, David and Emily, had been celebrating their silver wedding in Rome. It was their first visit, Emily had always wanted to see the Roman sights, and they had booked into the Hotel Universal – two star, central, no restaurant, not ruinously expensive – for a fortnight. But Emily's father, a widower, Billy Williams by name, had fallen ill on the day after they left home. Archibald Crisp, son of David and Emily, had broken the news on the second day of the Crisps' holiday, and Archie had rung his mother, or his mother had had rung him on all the other days. At last Emily had yielded to the pressure and cut her holiday short by twenty-four hours.

Emily had always been good, a good girl, good daughter, wife and mother, and David was aware that he was the main beneficiary of her goodness. She was nothing like her only sibling, her elder sister Jane, at present footloose in South America after two childless marriages and two divorces. Emily had proved her differences over and over again, rushing to the rescue of children as well as parents, and ever ready to support David. He appreciated her, he boasted of his luck in the matrimonial game of chance, he told her and other people that he did not deserve her.

He nonetheless wished she had not reacted as she did to her father's latest health scare – over-reaction, as he saw it. Billy Williams' heart had withstood several attacks; he was in the hands of cardiac specialists, he took their pills, followed their instructions in respect of diet and exercise, and was being considered for the insertion of a pacemaker and a bypass operation. He was unlikely to come to much harm, and, in David's opinion, liked to be fussed over by his daughter, as he had been by his wife, Marigold. Emily's dilemma, whether or not to act the Samaritan this time round, had overshadowed nearly all the Crisps' precious days in Rome, and they had wasted hours on telephone calls to their travel agency and in ticket offices. David liked Billy and had stopped short of saying he was a hypochondriac and spoilsport; but his simmer of irritation heated up now that Emily had gone and left him in a strange city of her choosing for their silver wedding treat.

It was not right, he thought. She had vowed in church to love him 'forsaking all others'. For once, she was not good. And in the circumstances, because she seemed to him to have stepped outside the sacrosanct circle of their marital obligations, he ventured into an area of revelatory light and receding frontiers.

The time was nine-thirty, and he sat in the empty lounge of the hotel and pretended to read a copy of yesterday's *New York Herald Tribune*.

How long ago their courtship had been in his recollection! He was working at Macer and Underwood, Estate Agency, she was the receptionist at a car showroom in Piccadilly. They were both in their early twenties, living with their parents in the village of Five Oaks, a suburb of Richmond upon Thames. They met at a local dance. She was pretty and vital, he was straight and susceptible – a dance or two was their undoing. Permissiveness had not reached Five Oaks, they were virgins, and had kept sex at bay with her games of badminton and his rugger and cricket. There was a rather wild necking session one night after he had taken her to a movie – it was in somebody's carport round the corner from her home. A couple of dress or rather undress rehearsals when they had his home to themselves, strong-minded on her side, frustrating on his, pushed his impatience to the point at which he proposed. They married, and then a child, Archibald soon nicknamed Archie, barged in or out, followed by Gwen.

The lounge was empty. It was a space at one side of the passage running from the front door of the hotel to the back alley, not a proper room; and the American and Japanese residents were already out on the tourist trail. David shook his newspaper as if to enable him to read it more easily, and still could not make sense of any of the print. He was ashamed to be thinking unkindly of Emily. She did not deserve criticism for not being able to resist pleas for her attention. He had often benefited from her sympathy, and it was mean to blame her for sympathising with another member of her family. David's shake of the newspaper had a side-effect, it shook the kaleidoscope of his reflections. He again saw his wife in her angelic guise, lovable and still attractive, and doing her best to cope with sorrows and share joys.

She had not trapped him, she never had. They had conformed to the way of the world, and followed the dictates of nature. He was desirous of her treasure, and after he had vowed to love her for ever she let him have it. No, it was nothing like that, not blackmail, not materialistic! They had loved each other, and consummated their love with God's approval. And they had been happy, had hardly ever quarrelled for twenty-five years, neither of them looking to right or left, surviving the seven year itch, a model pair and well-meaning parents.

But the years of paternity had been hard and long, if not so hard for him as motherhood was for Emily. He supported her, he did his bit, and he was supported, and learned lessons, one in particular. She was a more wilful mother than wife. She expected, demanded, more from their children's father than from her husband. There was iron in the soul of the jolly amenable girl he had wed. Inexperience, sleepless nights, toil at the money mill, sheer exhaustion were no excuses in her maternal eyes. He admired her devotion to Archie and Gwen, and her tirelessness. He was eventually grateful that she had compelled him not to throw in the towel. After all, he was proud to have reared his dutiful son and to be the grandfather of Anna – Gwen was another matter.

He shied away from painful thoughts of his daughter.

Here he was in Rome, kicking his heels, without Emily to drag him to another church, to see another holy picture, and to walk miles!

A different response to his twenty-four hours of loneliness was available. He would be alone in the historical home of the more or less deadly sins, in a manner of speaking or thinking. Fidelity had not blinded his eyes to the temptations of the female form, and in Rome he had suffered from exchanges of glances with knowing black eyes, from being caught out staring at goods that were out of reach – caught luckily not by Emily. Italian girls were ready and willing to make exhibitions of themselves, like the girl in the miniskirt in the *Vicolo Garibaldi*, and they seemed to take a cruel delight in showing how intimate they were with the buttocks of their lovers. The pictures and statues of naked women he had seen in museums and galleries drew his attention less to art than to the female flesh and blood he was nearly bumping into in the city streets.

He was a shop-keeper, he sold houses, not an aesthete. Emily, ever since the children were at school and began to grow up, had dabbled in art. She attended a weekly drawing class and on another weekday threw pots. They had pictures painted by her on the walls of 12 Manor Crescent, and sometimes drank out of her weighty pottery teacups. She liked coffee-table art books and pored over the pictures. It was mainly for art's sake that they had come to Rome, and, consequently, spent hours gazing at martyrdoms and crucifixions.

Again, David recoiled from the unfairness of his resentment. He himself had suggested Rome in order to please Emily. He was interested to learn about the Renaissance, he especially admired Leonardo's drawings of machines. He always had regret that his chief preoccupation was money, earning enough to feed his family, and he was missing out on higher things, art and proper music. He had thought Rome might be a step in a new and rewarding direction, and now he was wishing Emily had offered to accompany him to a bar with pole-dancing or a night club with a raunchy cabaret.

He shook his paper. He must get out in the fresh air and let the sun warm the cockles of his heart. He was more at fault because he could have changed his ticket and held Emily's hand in the aeroplane. He could have offered her a shoulder to cry on when she had visited her father. Instead, he had drawn the line at sacrifices for relations. There had been too many, he had too many defunct members of his own family, uncles and cousins, his late mother-in-law Marigold. He had dug in his toes at last, for once, and said he was not going to pay for a hotel room that was unoccupied or swap a day of his holiday for the stresses and strains of what was more than likely another of Billy's false alarms.

He replaced the newspaper, went along to the front door, tested the temperature, climbed the stairs to the room on the first floor – the twin beds had not been made up, and the sight of Emily's caused David a variety of pangs – collected his panama hat and in due course sallied out into the streets.

He was heading for the *Basilica di San Pietro*, St Peter's. He knew the way there, they had visited it four times. Both Crisps were quite religious, that is, they were Christians, went to church when they could, and took Communion at Christmas and Easter. They had raised their children in the Christian faith. Actually, in Rome, David was impressed by the great straight road called Conciliazione leading to the Piazza with its colonnades, and then by the interior of the building, its size, height, statues, by its hordes of worshippers, many kissing the bronze toe of the statue of St Peter, and its picturesque guards in their historic uniforms. He was not averse to having another look at the place. Besides, considering his access of rebellious feelings for his beloved wife who had shown a preference for another man – her father – he thought he might be forgiven by higher authority in those holy surroundings, and, with luck, come to his senses.

But the sights he now saw, the Roman street

scene, affected him with an irresistible force. Girls arm-in-arm looked at him boldly as they swaggered by. A single saucy teenager blew him a kiss. Couples were entwined in each other's arms. A woman was singing a love song while she hung out sheets on a clothes line stretched between two first floor windows. In another open upstairs window a female was combing and drying in the sun the long black hair she had washed. He had not noticed all the carnality before, he had not let himself; perhaps Emily somehow put a lid on it. Her absence, and his chafing against her rule, meant that he entertained stirring thoughts. These living members of the opposite sex appealed to his rudimentary ideas of beauty more than portrayals of women and marble statues.

He was not a sex-starved husband. He could not pretend for a moment that Emily had short-changed him in that context. At the same time he remembered his realisation that there was another world of sexual experience that he and she had not explored and never would. He read books about it, not deliberately – it was touched upon and hinted at in some of the novels he and Emily took out of the Public Library. A sort of rutting season, sex anywhere, at any hour of the day or night, on impulse, and causing life-changing and death-defying explosions of sensation, was nothing like their brief and regular communing at bedtime. Even on their honeymoon love had expressed itself with dignity and reserve. After the children were born, and in subsequent years, intercourse had been less frequent. Now because they were at a distance from each other, she by choosing to abandon him, he by exceptionally finding fault with her, his secret fantasies and fancies escaped from whenever they had been locked away.

He strolled more slowly towards St Peter's. The Italian temperament in action seemed to be unravelling his English inhibitions. His roving eyes passed over the respectable ladies of a certain age in their neat black garments and the gentlemen in sober suits and discreet ties, and picked out the nubile forms, the red lips, the skin that was not pink and white, the living temptations confident and provocative on their high heels.

He crossed the Tiber by the bridge called Emanuelle and was in sight of the road that leads to the Basilica. He stopped there. He had associated the Tiber with the Rubicon. He did not want to go to church, he admitted it. The last thing he was wanting was church, and he could not be blamed for his nature. He meant no harm, he intended nothing stupid, he never had; he was the co-proprietor of Macer and Crisp – he had bought Mr Underwood's shares five years ago. He was not any old fool, he would and was able to control himself – anyway, he had not much money on him. He simply wanted to lap up the atmosphere of love that was free, of the country of sunshine and oranges. He would be a spectator, not a player of the most ancient of all sports invented by Adam and Eve.

He walked away from St Peter's, towards the

Castel San Angelo, crossed another bridge and was back in the part of Rome in which the Hotel Universal was located. He had an urge to be off thoroughfares and rid of shoppers, and turned into narrow roads and alleys between high old buildings with blackened walls. He was in a run-down area behind a rich one, a slum inhabited by shifty men, tired women, grubby children and stray dogs. His finding himself there, in unsuitable surroundings, not where Emily would wish him to be, a squalid sink of iniquity in her probable opinion, fitted in with his notion that he was now on the wrong yet desirable side of the Rubicon.

He lost his way almost on purpose. He was intrigued by open doorways revealing dark stone staircases to upper floors. Old people sat in some open doorways, women knitting or shouting at deaf men sitting opposite. Boys on motorbikes raced through. He came across an unhygienic butcher's shop, and a greengrocer's selling fruit and veg looking the worse for wear.

Time had passed: out of an entrance to a house with a curtain of sacking for a door, smells of food cooking emanated. David felt a pang of hunger. Shoppers carrying loaves of fresh bread three feet long tempted him in a different direction. He noticed a sign on the pavement bearing the legend, *Spaghetti e Vino*. He peeped into a hot smoky room with a few men sitting on benches. They wore T-shirts and builders' soiled trousers, and had hairy chests and forearms. He was shy of entering with his brass-buttoned blazer and creased cavalry twills, and bad Italian. But he was not a coward, he strode in, wished the men good day, sat at a table by himself, and a forbidding female slapped down a basket of bread, a glass of red wine, and then a bowl of spaghetti with tomato sauce.

He ate with relish, enjoyed the wine that burned his throat, paid with his pocket money, said his goodbyes and resumed his peregrinations.

At three o'clock he was in the square of the Pantheon. He had eaten at midday, had been walking for hours, and the sun was still hot and high. He sat at a table in front of one of the cafés and asked a waiter for a lemon drink with sugar. He had had a nicer time than might have been the case. He had succeeded in having an adventure, judging by his somewhat puritanical standards. He watched the girls in a mood of reluctant resignation, looking at the pillared front of the Pantheon – he thought he might have another look at the mysterious interior later on. His lemon drink arrived, and a woman bumped into his table.

There was an apologetic exchange. She had long dark brown very curly hair. She was young middle age. He expected her to move away, but she put a hand on his table as if to steady herself, and looking him in the face asked in a faint voice: 'Can I sit down?'

He rose to his feet, pushed a chair towards her, offered her assistance and said he was sorry.

She sat with her head bowed, and her long hair fell in front of her face. She was English, which made communication easier.

13

'Are you all right?'

'Oh yes,' she replied, and then looked up and straight at him, smiling.

'Do you need help?'

'No, no.' Her face was pretty, her smile appealing. 'Would you give me a hand to where I want to go?'

He hesitated. She was not a nondescript stranger. They seemed to be alone in the crowd, isolated together.

She hung her head and took two gasping breaths, she was clearly ill and in trouble.

'Yes,' he said. 'Is it far from here?'

'Not far.'

'I'll take you there.'

'Oh thank you.'

He waited. Her head was bowed. He wondered if he would be walking into a trap. But he was a man of experience. He could cope with narrow squeaks. And Emily could not object.

'I'm so sorry.'

The voice was soft verging on intimate. The accent was educated verging on high class. She was wearing brightly coloured clothes. She again looked up and into his eyes with hers, which were blue, humorous, inviting, involving.

'You haven't finished your drink,' she said.

'Are you feeling better?'

'Yes. What about your drink?'

'It doesn't matter.'

'Really?'

'I'll take you home.'

They stood up. She led the way through the

tables and chairs. In the square she linked her arm in his either to support herself, or guide him, or for an ulterior motive. He hoped no friend or acquaintance would happen to be about and to see him with a woman who was not his wife on his arm. She turned into a backstreet, and then another – he lost his way. They talked a little, but she was now short of breath.

'Will you need a doctor?'

'Oh no! I'm very strong.'

She gave his arm a squeeze to prove it.

'You're a kind man, a gentleman,' she said, 'and you're strong, too – I can feel it. What's your name?'

After a wary second or two he answered, 'David.'

'David suits you.'

'What's yours?'

'My name is Carmen.'

She said it as if it had been a quotation.

'Are you Spanish?'

'Yes – and no.'

She laughed spontaneously, he followed suit, her ambiguous answer was not explained.

'Where are we?'

The alley was sordid, full of bulging black bags, garbage bins, spilt refuse, and overshadowed by more high buildings from which metal fire escapes angled down.

'Here,' she said, releasing his arm and descending by steep steps into a basement area where she opened a door. 'Come in for a minute!'

He did not need to, and should not, but he was curious, polite, caring, magnetised, unable to resist.

It was one room, a bed-sitting-room, sparsely furnished with a bed and cushions and a table and two chairs. A single grubby window did not admit much light.

'This isn't your home,' he said.

'For today only. Come and sit down.' She took his hand and led him to a chair – they both sat at the table.

'I must go.'

'No, please, I would be so grateful if you'd stay with me. Nobody's in a rush in the afternoons in Rome. Would you like a drink of water?' She laughed at her inadequate hospitality. 'I want to repay you.'

'Don't think of that.'

'But I am thinking. Give me your hand and I'll pay you not in money. Don't be afraid!'

'You're a strange person.'

'Sometimes it's nice to be strange together. Give me your left hand!'

'What for? Why?'

'Wait and see.'

He did as he was told – her will was stronger than his. She reached across, held his hand between both of hers, which were warm and soft, and fondled it while she gazed into his eyes. The expression on her face, and slightly parted lips, was daring, playful, questioning, asking him to be tolerant and conspiratorial. He realised what she was doing, and let her do it. She had removed the wedding ring Emily had put on his finger. She laid the ring on the brown wood of the top of the table. He said nothing, he was

16

too excited, bewitched, he could only watch the symbolical sensuality of her actions. Her hands were still on the table, and now she removed her own wedding ring and placed it next to his. They looked at each other like accomplices in a crime.

'Do you want to disappear?' she asked.

He jumped, he did not get her meaning, and was startled by the voice after the silence.

She pointed at a door into a washroom. He again obeyed her. It was primitive, a hole in the floor, a wash-basin and a bidet. When he came back, she took her turn in there, not fully closing the door. He waited for her in a sort of trance, concentrating on whatever might happen next, also on the room he was in, shutting out his life, his past. He was in the land of dreams. Flies buzzed up and down the windowpanes. He was tremendously excited.

She rejoined him. He stood, they faced each other, and she presented him with her knickers. He moved towards her, but she gestured to stop him, said 'Not yet!' with a little laugh. A plastic bag lay on the floor near the window; she went over to it, pulled out a fruit pie, smashed it against the wall, left it lying there, and explained, 'For the flies.' Then she began to undress him, and when he was naked she divested herself of her shirt, kicked off her shoes and let her skirt drop. She extended her left hand and took his, and led him to the bed.

The day advanced, the light through the window was dimmer. Appetites should have been more than satisfied; but appetite grows with eating. Before David and Carmen indulged in yet another rich course of their sexual feast, he paid a second visit to the washroom. When he emerged, she was lying on the bed with her back turned to encourage him. It was beautiful, the flexuous line of her spine, the shoulders fleshed out yet spare, no fat anywhere, and the perfect hips. He lay beside her, pressing his shape against hers. She was unresponsive.

He spoke her name. He thought she was asleep. But she was cold – he would cover her up. He fetched her clothes from where they lay on the floor, spread them over her, and saw her hand: the fingernails were blue. He realised that she could be very ill, and for the first time in these hours of madness a shaft of fear penetrated him from head to foot. He called her name and shook her. He turned her on to her back: there was no sign of life. He listened to her heart – nothing; he felt for a pulse – nothing; and no breath was detectable. He tried to give her artificial respiration, knelt over her, blew into her mouth, kneaded her heart with all his strength – nothing. She was dead. She was unmistakably and irreversibly dead.

CHAPTER TWO

David Crisp tried to pray. But the Lord's Prayer deteriorated into a meaningless moan of mingled terror and tears. He did not deserve favours from the Lord. It was too late to ask not to be led into temptation, and how could even the Almighty deliver him from the evil he had mixed himself up in? He was ashamed to pester God, he was hoping God had not noticed his goings-on. He wished he was a Roman Catholic, whose priests are invested with the power to absolve sinners. Yet to gain absolution he would have to confess everything, and he shrank like an anemone from the idea of telling anyone what he had done.

Oh, his misery – an emotion previously unknown except in name – a state of affairs reserved for sick souls and weaklings, he had believed – he had had no patience with the fashion for morbidity and blubbing over bad causes!

Oh God!

Again he forced himself to re-examine the woman on the rumpled coverlet of the bed – the material was brown towelling, washable towelling, he noticed. Squeamishly he remembered that he had worshipped her with his body minutes before, and vice versa, they had worshipped each other on the public convenience of a towel. Her eyes were closed, and her eye sockets were turning black. And her formerly red lips were white – she was black and white! Her hair still curled, but he doubted they were natural curls – surely hair loses its curl when blood does not reach it. She looked so woebegone, with her arms lying away from her body, that he placed her arms on her chest, folding them with difficulty below her pretty breasts. She was colder, and he hurried to spread her clothes all over the passionate person she had been. He covered her face for fear that it was somehow reproaching him.

He saw their rings on the table.

Her ring was like the thunderbolt that heralds the deluge – a deluge of realities in his case. He must put it back on her finger. And his ring was incriminating evidence. He returned his ring to the place it should never have left, on the third finger of his left hand; and struggled to do the same for Carmen – her finger was stiff already.

He realised he was prime suspect. How had she died? He did not know, but remembered the bruises his passion must have inflicted on her body, and that in some of their gymnastics he might have injured some part of her mortally. He could have killed her by accident. He could be thought to have murdered her. He was threatened by the laws of the land and by publicity, by having his name in international papers, by his family seeing his picture on a front page. He had intended to call an ambulance and the police:

mistakes! Innocence, ignorance, they always got people into trouble!

Even now he might be doing wrong to keep the medicos at bay – would they be able to revive her? And he certainly should inform the police. But he simply dared not risk any of that – he had to get out and get away with it if possible. He was not a criminal, he was the most law-abiding of men, yet he had to act as if he had committed a crime. Yes, the obvious conclusion to be jumped at was that the husband of a good wife and the father of a family had done the deed. Where to start? How to conceal his having been present when a woman died of a cause unknown?

He had nothing on. He climbed into his boxer shorts, shirt, trousers. He used a cotton sock as a cloth with which to wipe fingerprints off the table, chairs, the door of the washroom, the inner surface of the door into the street, the taps of the washbasin and the paraphernalia of the lavatory. He washed the soles of his shoes just in case, and took note of the flies, gorged on fruit pie, waddling about – he must take care not to step on any, nothing must connect him with the death scene.

He put on his socks and shoes. At last a pressing question occurred to him, a whole questionnaire. Who was Carmen? Where had they made love or lust? What was the bed-sitting-room, a flatlet, a hotel suite, a place she owned? How long before somebody came to investigate, to claim rent, to clean?

She had been a lady, although her behaviour was the opposite of ladylike. Her accent was not coarse, although she had uttered words in his ear that would have shocked a fishwife. She was clean, although she resorted to dirty tricks – kidnapping him, for instance. She was extremely beddable, why did she have to seek sex so urgently from a man in the street?

Half-answers were that she had been play-acting, assuming the name of a heroine of romance, copying the imaginary sexual antics of a fictional slut, and gaining the satisfaction that was denied her by circumstances of some description, because of an impotent husband, or an absent lover, or because she was terminally ill and out for a final throw of the dice. He could not believe she was often in the bed-sitting-room, it would have been less utilitarian if she had used it regularly. He had heard of day-rooms, rooms for rent in which people could copulate – they were mostly on the continent, he thought. Was their love-nest one of those? Anyway, her actions were premeditated – she had picked him up, escorted him to her parlour, and, in another nasty way of putting it, smashed him up like another sort of fruit pie so that her urgings would cease to bother her.

Escape was his next trial. He put on his blazer and hat, looked round the room once more, and, sentimentally in spite of his horrific preoccupations, checked the face of the woman who had given him thrills as well as terror. Something caught in his throat, an instant lump, at the same time his knees trembled, his legs went weak, he stumbled to a chair and sat with his head in his hands. He ached in his body and soul for Emily, for Gwen, for his grand-daughter Anna, his family, including himself. He saw in his mind's eye as if electronically: 'fast-forward' revealed that nothing was ever going to be the same, 'rewind' deleted the years of his aspiration to be a proper man, successful, happy.

Practicalities took over. He must not be arrested and tried in an Italian court for murder. He tiptoed to the door and turned the door-handle: it did not open, it was locked – she must have locked him in. Anger was strengthening. He hurried to the bed, now the bier, shook her clothes, searched for pockets, eventually found the key in a deep pocket in her skirt. He returned to the door, unlocked it quietly, wiped the key with the sleeve of his blazer, checked that his ring was on his finger, wiped his mouth with the back of his hand, stepped into the basement area, listened for a moment, mounted the steps and walked along the alley.

He was not stopped. Nobody shouted at or pursued him. He counted his slow strides to the end of the alley, and stepping to one side, so that he would be out of sight of anyone issuing from the building with the basement room, he removed his blazer and took off his hat. He then dared to steal a glance down the alley. It was empty. A sign on the building, on a sort of flagpole, was legible: *Albergo Diurno* – day hotel. He walked much faster along the street, glad to have to dodge other people, thankful for the protection, and saw a sign to the Pantheon and turned in the opposite direction.

The time on his wristwatch was six-thirty. He was too distraught to work out whether it would be later or earlier in Five Oaks. Darkness was falling, neon lit the city. He put on his blazer and hid his hat in a litter bin. Where to go? He walked where the neon lights were brightest and people congregated outside cafés, cinemas, bakers' shops, street vendors' stalls. A row between motorists attracted his attention, but the row was patched up. He had to remember the reason why he was wherever he was. He had not taken his map of Rome with him when he left the Hotel Universal, he had thought he would not need it on the glorious morning of his stroll towards St Peter's before he wrecked his life.

At seven-thirty he rested in a bus-shelter. His thoughts were like a family album. He saw Emily in her virginal youth, their wedding photographs, the christenings of Archie and Gwen, and the gathering at the lunch to celebrate the twenty-five years of his marriage. He was mourning the quarter of a century. Other men committed adultery without making a meal of it, as he was. His best friend Max had had extramarital affairs, and Max's wife Sheila had hit him on the head with a frying-pan the first time, and burned all his trousers the second; then they had kissed and made up. Max's vocation was to be a prodigal and a rascal; and Sheila was not too particular. David was not like Max – they were friends

24

because of their differences rather than their similarities. And Emily was nothing like Sheila, she thought Sheila was a foolish liberal. David had known almost as he allowed Carmen to steal his wedding ring that he was undermining his home and happiness. He studied the photographs in his memory as if they had been memorials.

Why had he done it? He had been hypnotised. It was the exception to his rule. He had been led like a lamb to the slaughter. He felt he would not be spared, and did not deserve to be.

He sat outside a café, at a table on the pavement, and ordered whisky for Dutch courage. He studied the passers-by, noting the change in his angle of vision. That morning, in broad daylight, his eyes had strayed to female curves, to the sweet inviting circularity of young womanhood; now, this evening, when lust had had its fill, he was drawn to the older couples holding hands or walking arm-in-arm, at peace with one another, not guilty.

The unintended consequence of the whisky was to make him feel light-headed. He walked on unsteadily. An illuminated statue on a plinth had been raised to honour soldiers who died in the line of duty. He was not dead, and even if he had not been dutiful or honourable he had to value his life. He smelt food, realised he had not eaten for hours, was obliged to pull himself together and try to serve nature. He read the menus outside modest restaurants, chose one that was not crowded, took a deep breath and entered. He ordered ravioli. He ate a little with difficulty, and a little more with hints of pleasure, then remembered and felt sick. When he was overcome by that last look at Carmen he had seized a chair and slumped on to it. He had left his fingerprints on the wooden structure and omitted to wipe them off. Whether it mattered, what likelihood there was of his being traced by a fingerprint or two and put in prison, all was overwhelmed by a great wave of fear and wretchedness.

At least it brought him face to face with priorities. Emily would be worried about him. And he had never rung to discover if she was safely back in Manor Crescent. And he had not been in the Hotel Universal in order to return a call she might have made. Mobile phones were beside the point: part of the treat of their holiday in Rome was that they would not take their mobiles. They had hoped not to be bothered for once by family problems, by Macer and Crisp, or by the hospital and the hospice where Emily volunteered to help. The telephone in their bedroom would be enough, they had told each other – in the event, it had been more than enough, for it led to summonses to come home without delay, to Carmen, adultery and catastrophe.

Subconsciously David had prolonged his way along his *via dolorosa* so as not to have to talk to Emily. She was more of a problem than prison, a more immediate one. When he looked at his watch yet again, and saw that it was past ten o'clock, he hoped it could be arguably too late to ring her or even return a call. But he was at fault for thinking of his wife so coldly, he was compounding his faults. He had to go back to the Hotel Universal sooner or later: ideas that he could either run away, into oblivion, or commit suicide, were discarded. He must be brave. It would be cruel to add even greater worries to the great ones he was going to cause her.

He asked a policeman for directions to the *Vicolo Garibaldi*. It was not close, he seemed to be told. The direction was to walk along a major road for several kilometres and then ask another policeman.

He did so, dragging his feet not on purpose but because they were as exhausted as he was. He reached the hotel shortly before midnight, still not knowing what the time would be in England. A night-watchman was on duty at the reception desk, David knew him by sight and that he was no linguist. The night-watchman handed him his room key and two slips of paper. He read them. They told a predictable story. He mounted the stairs and let himself into his, formerly their, bedroom. Emily's bed seemed to tick him off. He walked up and down the confined space, into the bathroom and back again. Could he wait for her to ring him? It would be her third call. The thought made him shudder: terrible that he was so in awe of the wife he had loved, he still loved; that he had become so faithless in a few hours; that he was a shadow of his former dominant self; that he had become a coward. He had to do the ringing – the hope that she might tire of trying to talk to him was vain and selfish. He had to get over the next of all the obstacles in his path.

He pressed the button on the room telephone for an outside line, and it buzzed strangely. He had not used Italian telephones much, was startled by the strangeness, and replaced the receiver. He walked some more, and at last, gritting his teeth, dialled the number of his home.

Before he could speak Emily asked in a panicky tone of voice: 'Are you all right?'

Her concern for him brought an enlarged lump into his throat, and he could not answer.

'David, David, are you there?'

'Yes,' he said; 'Yes – the line's bad.'

'What's happened?'

'Nothing.'

'Where have you been?'

'I'm sorry.'

'No – I'm relieved – I panicked, I couldn't help it, you weren't in our hotel.'

'No, I'm sorry, I'll explain. How's Billy?'

'He took a turn for the better – another turn – I needn't have left you.'

He fought back tears.

'David, can you hear me?'

'Yes.'

'Father's a bit better. I needn't have rushed home. I spoilt our holiday.'

'Not your fault,' he said in a strangulated type of voice.

'Are you well, my darling?'

'Yes, I think so.'

28

'What's wrong?'

'Nothing.'

'But your voice...'

'I stayed out too long in the night air.'

'Where were you?'

'Walking round Rome.'

'Not all day?'

'No, no.'

'Did you go back to St Peter's? You said you might.'

'Yes – in the morning – yes.'

He coughed in an attempt to dissolve the lump. He had told his wife a first lie.

'Was that nice? I was wondering what you were doing, and missing you and wishing I was with you.'

'I wished...'

'What did you say? I can't hear you well.'

'I wish you'd been with me.'

'Oh darling! Are you very tired? Do you want to sleep?'

'No.'

'Tell me about your day.'

'St Peter's was fine, as usual.'

'Did you have another look at our statue?'

She meant Michelangelo's *Pieta*, the statue of the seated Virgin Mary with the dead figure of her son Jesus lying across her knees.

'Yes,' he said, swallowed, and added: 'It made me sad again, it makes me sad.'

'Me too. Where did you have lunch? I just like to fill in the answers to my questions, where is he now, what's he doing? I'll stop if it's boring.'

29

'No. I ate in a spaghetti den somewhere near the Vatican.'

'Good food?'

'Yes, unexpectedly.'

'Not expensive?'

'Cheap.'

'Then?'

'I went into the Pantheon again. I wondered all over the place, and went into churches.'

'Where we'd been?'

'Yes.'

'What happened later, and this evening?'

'I had supper early – ravioli – very good.'

'Where?'

'I don't know.'

'Vaguely where?'

'Not far from the Colosseum.'

'You didn't go there? It's such a creepy place.'

'Yes, after supper – I met some people – I wanted to see the Colosseum at night, I'd read it was wonderful with floodlighting.'

'Who were the people you met?'

'Tourists.'

'A couple?'

'Yes – from America – New York. I stayed on talking to them, and forgot the time. Sorry, Emily.'

'Was it so wonderful?'

'In a way.'

'Not ghostly?'

'There were lots of tourists.'

'What were the Americans called?'

He hesitated.

'I don't know.'

'Didn't they call each other by name?'

'It was all terms of endearment, sweetiepie and honey.'

'They must have been quite amusing to keep you out so late. Wasn't it cold in the Colosseum?'

'Okay. I shouldn't have worried you. I'm no good without you. It's not been... It's not been a good day.'

'You're not feeling ill, David?'

'What makes you think that?'

'You don't seem to be yourself.'

'Who do I seem to be?'

She laughed.

He said: 'Tell me about your day.'

'It wasn't as interesting as yours.'

'How was the flight?'

'Safe – no alarms, thank goodness. Archie's Susan met me at Gatwick and drove me straight to St Christopher's to see Father. He knew us both and was fairly cheerful, considering.'

'A relief?'

'Yes.'

'Did you and Susan have lunch together?'

'I ate something more or less uneatable on the plane. Susan drove me to Manor Crescent, and hurried off to fetch Anna from kindergarten. She sent you her love. She'd shopped for me and left me rations. I threw out the junk mail and tidied the house, and eventually rang you.'

'Because I hadn't rung. I should have.'

'No "should" about it. Don't worry! I'm a bit envious of those Americans, but it's lovely to hear your voice, even if it sounds wonky. Has the hotel presented its bill?'

'It's a pleasure in store.'

'And I'm running it up with such a long telephone call.'

'It doesn't matter.'

'You'll have another early start in the morning, and you'll have the bill to pay as well as catching our flight. Would you like me to phone to make sure you're awake?'

'I'll manage, I won't oversleep.'

'It was such a heavenly holiday, David, thank you so much – and thank you, too, for saying I didn't absolutely spoil it. I think it was a rest cure for you after all your hard work, and will have done you good.'

'Yes, love.'

'You do feel better for it, don't you?'

'I probably will when I've had some sleep.'

'I'll meet you at Gatwick with the car.'

'No, please, darling – I'd rather be independent, I don't want you muddling about in those car parks.'

'Just as you like. Of course you're tired after so much walking. I'll let you go in a minute. Are you ready for bed?'

'Not quite.'

'I'm in bed and wish you were with me ... David?'

'I couldn't hear that, there's a fault on this line.'

'I said, we'll make up for lost time when you're back here with me. Do you understand?'

'Very well.'

'Safe journey, darling.'

'Thank you for everything, Emily.'

'Good night, sleep tight.'

'And you...'

She blew a kiss, and they rang off.

He was sweating. He was surprised that it had been so easy to lie and deceive her. How had she not noticed? Every word of their conversation turned the screw boring into his conscience, heart and soul. He stood in the open window for coolness, and tried to restrain his racing pulse.

He undressed himself this time, cleaned his teeth, washed thoroughly in the shower, went through all the motions of the routine of normality.

The future glowered at him. As for marital rights, they were unthinkable, and the prospect of difficulties in that area was beyond bearing.

He was getting into bed when it struck him – and it was like a blow below the belt. He had taken no precautions. Why had Carmen died, why was she unwell in front of the Pantheon, what was her illness, and had she infected him with it? The words that scared were syphilis and gonorrhoea, and then HIV, AIDS. He felt sick even to have them in his head. He was debarred by ethics, morality, written and unwritten rules, kindness, responsibility and humanity from touching Emily and from letting her touch him. How to prevent it? How to be tested? He could not consult John Tomkins, the family doctor and his friend.

The bells of Rome began to toll the hour. He

listened. He and Emily had loved the bells of Rome. They were ringing twelve times – midnight. They sounded like a knell.

CHAPTER THREE

Marriage is as mysterious as the beginning of life on earth. It can seem as mysterious to insiders as to outsiders. It has been called love, convenience, lust, commerce, compatibility and incompatibility, two halves of a whole, the art of compromise, the snake and ladder of snobbery, a glimpse of heaven or a sentence in hell.

David Crisp and Emily, née Williams, were happily married for a quarter of a century: everybody thought and said so. Quite a few of the common descriptions of successful matrimony were applicable to their union. They made vows before their God with sincerity and enthusiasm. They loved each other, they felt they did, and body added confirmation to soul. He was two years older than his wife; they had interests in common, and shared ideas of duty, ambition, friends and social ties. Sex was no problem, it oiled wheels, and children bridged gaps, children filled their free time. Their marriage was not far from being heavenly.

Where were the imperfections?

David was the only child of Hector, a cabinet maker and repairer of antique furniture, and Gloria, a teacher. The senior Crisps never saw much of their son, they were always busy, and David was a star-schoolboy, engaged in organised activities in terms and holidays; and after David married they saw him less. Nowadays Hector in his seventies still practised his craft, Gloria had retired. They were modest quiet people who lived in Saturn Street, off Maida Vale in the north of London, whereas David and Emily lived in the south. Hector presented his grandchildren with wooden toys he had made, Gloria with books that would help them to read and enjoy reading. David tried to remember to send them birthday cards, and Emily invited them to Manor Crescent for Christmas lunch. That was about that, except for the class difference.

Emily's father was Welsh, his people had been farmers in North Wales, but he married Marigold, who was born a Montgommery. Marigold's family lived in a large old house, a Welsh landmark, Montgommery Tower, and were involved in the administration and politics of the locality. Young Mr and Mrs Williams moved down to London, produced two daughters, Jane and Emily, and Marigold was a ladylike wife and mother while Billy went into the wine trade and made a career out of being popular.

The little girls' privileged upbringing and private education did not do Jane much obvious good, but Emily must have benefited. Women are sometimes compared to club sandwiches. The top layer of Emily was her touch of distinction, the next layer was her cleverness and know-how, the next her religion, charity, sympathy and kindness, the next an officer-like quality and a trace of high-handedness; and the final layer her wish to have her own way, the right way as she saw it.

David was a good businessman and a hard worker. He was also a dominant male, he wore the trousers – Emily was apt to say so. But whenever they came to a crossroads in their marital life, she read the map. He did not object, she was too tactful to draw attention to her leadership – he was subconsciously thankful to be relieved of a responsibility. They would have agreed wholeheartedly that they had reason to celebrate their silver wedding. The strains of parenthood, the stress of crises, the death of Marigold, the elopement of Gwen, had cemented their relationship.

David Crisp, during the flight from Rome to Gatwick, felt crushed by the weight of recent events, by memories, and by his experience of his wife's character. He was so afraid of hurting Emily. He was afraid, period. He had had an awful night in the Hotel Universal. He could not control the wildness of his mental processes. Sex would not let him go. He was torn in two by remembering Carmen's sexual inventiveness and ingenuity, and looking ahead to relatively straitlaced life with Emily. Anyway, he should not make love to her, perhaps ever again, whether or not he actually could.

How much had she suspected on the telephone? How was he to defend himself? How to protect her?

He drank whisky instead of eating the uneatable food on offer, and was the more alarmed by seeing his hand shake.

Luckily, Emily was not at Gatwick: he had half expected her to meet him there despite his plea to the contrary. He travelled by public transport and quicker by taxi to Manor Crescent. She opened the door before he rang the bell, and welcomed him with smiles and open arms. She shut the door and in the front hall tried to kiss his lips. He held her at arm's length and asked: 'How's Billy?'

'Alive,' she answered, 'still alive,' and pulled him closer.

He resisted and said: 'My darling, I have something to explain. Yesterday…'

'What's happened?' she interrupted with alarm and crinkled brow.

'Nothing, nothing much, bug trouble.'

'What?'

'I've caught a bug or a bug's caught me.'

'Since when?'

'Since yesterday.'

'You didn't tell me when I rang.'

'No—'

'I knew there was something wrong.'

'It's nothing much. I hoped it would go away.'

'What do you mean? What is it?'

'It's affected my waterworks.'

'How?'

'I'd rather not talk about it – let's change the subject.'

'Shall I ring up Dr Tomkins?'

'No, for heaven's sake, Emily! It's a minor infection of some sort, and it'll clear of its own accord.'

'Dr Tomkins—'

David interrupted.

'Dr Tomkins will give me an antibiotic, I'm not taking antibiotics for nothing, and I'm not dragging in the medical profession yet. What I'm trying to explain is that I'm not going to pass the infection on to you.'

'Poor darling – thank you, but—'

'No buts – I'm sorry – I'll be better soon.'

'Are you in pain?'

'No.'

He gasped involuntarily because the lie stuck in his throat.

'Are you feeling bad? You haven't got a temperature, have you?'

'No, no.'

'What do you want me to do? I've made plans. Sue's bringing Anna here for tea, and I've invited people to meals, and we've been invited.'

'It's business as usual.'

'You'd like to see Sue and our grandchild, wouldn't you?'

'My plan was to look in at the office. I'll unpack and pop along to the office, and try to get back in time to see Anna. Are we alone this evening?'

'We could be. Archie said he might look in for a drink. Shall I put him off?'

'You do as you please, that'll be okay.'

'What a horrid thing to happen to you! Have you ever had it before?'

'No.'

'Cystitis is awful for women, I know, though I've never had it, but I didn't think men get cystitis.'

'The point is that kisses are out for the time being.'

'I'm sure I'd be immune.'

'No, not worth risking it – sorry again.'

'Would you like a cup of tea or anything? I suppose you ate on the plane?'

'I did. No, thanks, nothing to eat. I'll do my unpacking if that's okay.'

'Are you pleased to be home, dearest?'

'Very much so.'

He climbed the stairs and was breathless when he reached his walk-in clothes cupboard. Lying took his breath away. He had not done badly by selfish reckoning; but was churned up inside by the shock of estranging himself from his wife. He could not warm to her. He saw her more as an opponent. What was not bad was also worse and worse.

He bade her goodbye and left the house. The walk to Macer and Crisp took ten minutes: it was slightly restorative. He was reunited with his fellow directors, Joe Macer and Anne Wake, and Polly, the receptionist. He told them he had had a great time in Rome, they told him the business had been good in his absence. They handed over printouts, and he retired into his exclusive sanctum – the others sat at desks in the open shop-floor.

He looked in his address book and dialled a telephone number.

'Max,' he said, 'it's David.'

He was speaking to his friend Max Harrison, the libertine, now wifeless and apparently going straight businesswise in an obscure Hedge Fund called Gilding the Lily.

'Hi,' Max replied.

'I need advice.'

'You need advice, I'm accustomed to asking you for the advice.'

'I'm in a fix.'

'Good heavens, what is the world coming to?'

'Can you talk confidentially?'

'Yes, if I press a button. Okay – what's up?'

'Where can I get a test for sexually transmitted disease?'

'What the hell have you of all people been at?'

'I might have caught it.'

'Join the club!'

'I can't pass on anything, I simply can't.'

'Didn't you wear a slipper?'

'No.'

'You're too innocent to go abroad.'

'Come on, Max!'

'Not flattering that you should think I know a man who can get adulterers out of jail! Okay – he's called Yonak, Dr Yonak. He has premises in North London, he's competent and trustworthy, and costs a basic two hundred and fifty in cash.'

'Oh dear, cash! Emily and I have joint bank accounts.'

41

'Couldn't you raid the petty cash box?'

'Possibly.'

'I could advance the money.'

'Thanks, Max, but no. Is the Doctor's surgery crammed with invalids? I don't want to meet people who know me or I know.'

'You won't. He's discreet. He'll know the reason why and see you in the middle of the night, specially if you mention my name.'

'What's the address?'

It was in Camden, near a Tube station. David thanked Max again.

Max replied: 'Good luck! A bit on the side isn't a big deal. We live in permissive days, and women take the pill. Be brave, old boy!'

Alone, partitioned off from colleagues and the rest of the world, David plotted. He counted the money in his wallet secretively, and jotted down figures on a scrap of paper he then put in his pocket. He summoned Joe Macer and asked if he could have a hundred pounds out of the till – he had a friend who owed it to a bookmaker. Joe produced the money. David left the office, saying he would be back to work on the next day, and walked to the only red telephone box in Five Oaks, where he dialled the number Max had given him.

A cultivated voice with Oxford accent said: 'Dr Yonak, can I help you?'

'Thank you, Doctor, yes, you could – I want to be tested for infections.'

'You're not my patient?'

'No.'

'How did you come by my telephone number?'

'Max Harrison told me.'

'I see. Max is a very private man.'

'So am I.'

'My fee for private consultation is two hundred and fifty pounds in the hand in advance.'

'I know.'

'How urgent are your tests?'

David hesitated before saying, 'Very' – a quick all-clear was desirable, the alternative was unthinkable.

'I could fit you in this afternoon at four sharp. Would that suit?'

'Yes.'

'You have my address?'

David read it out, Dr Yonak confirmed it and issued a few directions, and they rang off.

David walked along to the Covered Market, a noted feature of Five Oaks, an old railway shed offering space to stall-holders selling food, clothing, jewellery and so on. It attracted foreign tourists, and there was a kiosk dealing in currencies. David exchanged his euros for fifty-six pounds sterling, and at an ATM, a hole in a shed rather than in a wall, he withdrew fifty pounds from the Crisps' household account. He had another sixty pounds left over from the cash he had taken abroad, therefore had two hundred and sixty-six pounds in his pocket. He caught a train to Central London and a bus to Camden.

In the bus he reflected that at least he was taking positive action and had covered his tracks. His second thought was that he had almost become a criminal. His third and subsequent thoughts revolved round the degradation of the man he had been not so long ago.

Yet again, out of the shadows, emerged the ghost of the woman in the *Albergo Diurno* in a Roman backstreet on a Roman afternoon. He could not stop himself marvelling at the beauty of her sensitive and sensual body. Why had she died, and so suddenly? He had scarcely granted her death a minute of his attention while he fretted and fumed about his life.

He yanked his ruminations back to Emily. He tried to concentrate on the imminent demise of Billy Williams. He derived a mite of comfort from the argument that he was doing his best to shield his family from the effects of his infidelity.

Dr Yonak opened the door and led the way into a consulting room looking suspiciously like an operating theatre. He was a brown-faced man with silver hair in a white coat. He indicated a large leather chair under a bright light, and David sat down, produced the money, and obeyed instructions to remove the jacket of his suit and roll up the right sleeve of his shirt. The doctor put on rubber gloves, inserted a needle in a vein, drew blood out and put it into a number of different glass containers. He said he would test for all diseases of a sexual nature, and that the expense was due to the required anonymity of the patient. He told David to ring again at such and such a time in one week.

Back in the bus David was fearful of everything,

the result of the tests, the week ahead, possibly a future of keeping Emily at arm's length, and the resumption of so-called normal life in which he would feel and be abnormal.

Halfway down Marylebone Road he got off the bus and went into a shop he had spotted, a newsagent's. He looked amongst the foreign newspapers and bought a copy of an Italian one, *La Repubblica.* He hurried round a corner, into a quieter street, and searched in page after page of the paper for a report of a foreign woman who had died in a short-stay hotel. He found nothing, but was not relieved: the report could have been in yesterday's issue or would be in tomorrow's.

He was late home, he had lingered, not particularly wanting to see an eighteen-month old baby even if she was his grand-daughter, nor to listen to Susan, his daughter-in-law, boasting about the perfection of her husband, Archie. He just caught a glimpse of them in their car, Sue wound down the window and called out to him, 'So glad you had such a smashing time in Rome!' He smiled at her and signalled agreement: 'smashing' was not a bad description of the time he had had.

The rest of that day was fraught, although the Crisps were spared the company of Archie. Emily spoke of her father. She had visited him in his hospice – the St Christopher's Hospice where she worked intermittently – in the course of the afternoon. He had revived to some extent. He had been terminal a few days ago, today he was up, dressed, sitting with the other invalids, and laughing. She had been pleasantly surprised; but it would not last. David would have to seize his chance to see Billy. He would have to go soon. The question was when?

David ground his teeth metaphorically. He was fond of Billy, but not in the mood to have Billy forced down his throat. That her parents took precedence was an old bone of contention. For the sake of peace he had neglected his own father and mother – his mother-in-law had had to be entertained and visited, and now it was her father's turn. Emily meanwhile was answering her own question: four o'clock tomorrow afternoon would do, he would not clash with other expected visitors. He obediently wrote the time of the appointment in his diary, thinking: for goodness sake, I can't cope with secondary issues!

He just remarked: 'I'll have to visit my parents soon, too.'

'Oh well,' she replied, 'can't I leave that to you? They're not dying.'

She dictated other entries for his diary. She had invited the Johnsons and Whitakers to dinner on such and such a day, and poor old Molly Fishburn to tea on another. Archie, Susan and little Anna were coming to lunch on Sunday. She was concerned never to have Joe Macer and his wife Mandy in the house: they were such nice people and he was such a good colleague for David.

'Yes, yes,' he said. 'Some time – I agree – yes, do – suits me,' he said.

He too had been hospitable, he was proud of his wife's accomplishments as hostess: now he thought, 'Frivolity, triviality!' He excused himself, went upstairs, ran a bath, and lying in it yearned as never before for peace and quiet, for innocence, and to be not himself.

The doorbell rang. He heard cries, laughter, shrieks of laughter, and a raucous voice, a recognisable voice – Jane's, his sister-in-law's. He groaned. She was not invited, she had not warned anybody, she was calling without permission, typically, selfishly, and he could have killed her – well, not killed, but thrown her out into the street and slammed the door in her face. He was not equal to Jane, certainly not this evening, if ever. She expected supper, of course, and possibly to stay the night: she would bellow and boast, and there would be an inevitable row with Emily. A thought of another brighter colour struck him. He was disloyal, he was bad to think it, but the fact was that she would be a buffer. He climbed out of his bath and prepared for the fray.

Jane screamed at the sight of him and ran into his arms. She called him 'gorgeous', and embraced him tightly. Their relations had always consisted of false flirting. Emily frowned and raised her eyes to heaven behind her sister's back. Jane was saying that she had hurried 'home' to see her father, and was so grateful for having been offered 'a bed' for however long the tragic vigil lasted. David said he had seen her overnight bag, an ironical reference to the bulging suitcases in the hall, and she giggled and shook her fist at him.

They adjourned to the kitchen, and trouble was not long delayed. Emily shared her steak with Jane unwillingly, and Jane told David that his wife was a nice little cook. Then Jane knew more about Gwen than her parents knew, they apparently communicated by e-mail. She said that David and Emily ought to forgive Gwen, which elicited furious denials from Emily that her daughter had ever been unforgiven. David had to censor that topic of conversation: 'Leave Gwen out of it, please!' Jane regaled them with traveller's tales of her high life in the casinos of Las Vegas, the beaches of Rio, the slopes of Aspen, and gave saucy accounts of the suitors who had paid her bills. Towards the end of the meal – and the evening, David hoped – the sisters clashed head to head over the relic of their father.

Jane began it by saying she had already seen him in the hospice.

'I spent half an hour by his bedside before coming here.'

Emily burst out: 'What? How could you do that without consulting me! I've been in charge of all his visits. And half an hour's far too long, he'll have another collapse.'

'Well, he seemed to be enjoying himself, we had a laugh together,' Jane retorted.

'Let's wait and see how much damage you've done. Ignorance is bliss. How could you know anything? You haven't been near Dad for years.'

'Better late than never, dear.'

'I don't know about that. Why are you in Five

Oaks? I agree it's convenient timing, just in time for the will.'

'Sorry if you're scared I'll nab some of the cream before you've lapped it all up.'

'I'm not a money-grabber, I'm nothing like you, Jane, thank God!'

'No, you're huffy, you always were, and I'm not.'

'Oh, I hate you, I do!'

'Snap!'

David intervened. He told the truth when he said: 'I can't stand any more of it.'

He pushed back his chair and got to his feet, and the women followed suit. Jane said she was dog-tired – 'bitch-tired', she corrected herself – and that if David would be kind enough to help with her luggage she would make it an early night. Emily said she would do the same after clearing up the mess in the kitchen, and Jane had the typical last word: instead of offering to help, she said with a wink at David, 'We've all got our books to read, haven't we?'

Emily was crying when David returned to the kitchen. He tried to concentrate on comforting her. They did the washing up together. At last she took pity on his supposed indisposition, shooed him up to bed, and followed not long afterwards.

He switched off his bedside lamp and lay with his eyes closed. He was worn out – by everybody and everything – he longed for the oblivion of sleep. Emily completed her ritual at the dressing table, looking at herself in the mirror, and

49

eventually got into her bed. Instead of reading, she also switched off her light.

'Are you awake?' she asked quietly.

He resigned himself to replying, 'Yes.'

'I shouldn't have left you alone in Rome.'

'You felt you had to go, I understood you.'

'I'm sorry about Jane.'

'She'll be off soon – Billy has no money to speak of.'

'She's nowhere to go to.'

'That's her fault.'

'Thank you for marrying me, David.'

'It's the other way round.'

There was a pause. He somehow knew she was not sleeping. He started to say, 'Thank you...' but was choked by the lump in his throat.

'Are you ill?' she asked.

'No.'

'But your trouble, is that better?'

'Not yet – perhaps a little.'

'Will you see Dr Tomkins?'

'If it doesn't go away.'

'It's not serious, is it?'

'No.'

'What is it?'

'I don't know – I'm trying to forget it.'

There was another silence.

She said: 'I wish you didn't have an infection.'

'So do I.'

'Can we make love again?'

'Of course.'

'Promise?'

'Yes.'
'Are you tired?'
'A bit.'
'Do you mind if I read?'
'No.'
'Good night, dearest.'
'Good night.'

CHAPTER FOUR

He slept in the end, it must have been at one or two the next morning, he slept without remembering, and was roused by Emily at their accustomed hour, seven o'clock.

She was asking him: 'Are you going to work?'

'Yes! He was instantly in a panic. 'What's the time?'

She told him.

'Yes, I must get on, thanks for waking me.'

He shaved and washed, donned his grey suit, read the newspaper while he ate his breakfast of a slice of toast, told Emily he would come home at three or thereabouts in the afternoon preparatory to visiting Billy, and kissed her goodbye.

It was routine, reassuringly humdrum, and meant, for David in his special circumstances, escape.

Work in the office was also soothing. He was busy non-stop, talking to customers wanting to buy or sell property, viewing a flat that might be put on the market, escorting a couple to a house they were interested in, and pleased to be making money. He was pleased to be a robot, not a nervous wreck. The ringing of the telephone on his desk did not threaten him with heart failure. Rome was miles away, he was in Macer and Crisp in the High Street of Five Oaks, and his profile was so low as to be almost at vanishing point. The thought he held about the recent past was that he might be out of range of being sucked back into it.

At one-thirty in the afternoon he met a Mr Wilkinson at a property not far from the office, a maisonette over a shop in the High Street. The vendor was abroad, David had the key, he showed Mr Wilkinson round, and they parted – Mr Wilkinson had been non-committal. David had an hour to fill before he would be expected at Manor Crescent, and was disinclined to return to the office. He noticed the library down a side street and was drawn towards it. He had not been bothered by Carmen during the day, but he suddenly wanted information, to know more about her and her name.

He spoke to a girl officiating in the front hall of the premises. He was not inhibited, not a reader and not acquainted with the library staff, he did not mean to incriminate himself, and on impulse was ready to run the risk.

'Can you tell me anything about "Carmen" – is it a book?' he inquired.

'It's an opera,' the girl replied.

'Was it a book before it was an opera? Books are made into operas, aren't they?'

'I could look it up for you.'

'Would you mind?'

'No problem.'

She pressed buttons and peered into her computer screen.

'Oh yes,' she said. 'Here we are! It's a book all right, French, in lots of translations, and we used to have it, but it's not on the latest register. If you go up to the second floor and look at "Foreign", you might find a copy amongst the old books.'

He followed her advice. The second floor was a maze of iron bookshelves full of dusty books. There was a strong smell of dust, and nobody there. He found 'Foreign' and then *Carmen*, and finally a table and chair with a light to read by.

The volume was slim. The author was Mérimée, the translator not credited, and the date of publication the mid-twentieth century. The story did not begin at once, the author wrote about archaeology, and David skipped. Unexpectedly, the archaeologist was describing the gipsy Carmen in the cigar factory and seducing a soldier, Don Jose. David skipped on. She buys a fruit pie as they go to her dwelling, 'for the flies'. Don Jose is obsessed with Carmen, deserts the army and joins her gang of smugglers. But she tires of him, she falls in love with a matador, will have nothing to do with Don Jose, who is ruined, mad with jealousy, and murders her.

David shut the book, replaced it and left the library. He was shaken. His Carmen had acted *Carmen* and cast him in the role of Don Jose. But his Carmen was dead, he could not get more obsessed with her than he was, and he did not have to murder her for whatever she had been doing. The uncanniness scared him nonetheless. What had he been involved in? He was not too surprised, he had thought she was pretending to be someone else, namely Carmen in a romantic tale; but had she planned to provoke him into stabbing her to death?

He walked and adjusted his breathing. He was trying to be in the right frame of mind, fit for attending the deathbed of his father-in-law. He studied his watch – he must not make matters worse by keeping Emily waiting.

He was not late at Manor Crescent. He drove Emily to St Christopher's, and he followed her directions to the room Billy was in – she was going to seek out and obtain information from nurses. David saw Billy through the open door of his room, asleep in a chair, wearing pyjamas, dressing-gown, large furry slippers, his thin hair disarrayed, his head lolling forwards and sideways in an unnatural position. He was distressingly nothing like the smart commanding sort of man he had been. David tiptoed in and sat on a wooden chair.

After three or four minutes Billy woke, blinking, seeing his visitor, straightening up his head, smiling and saying: 'Glad you had a good time in Rome.'

His voice was weak. Their ensuing conversation was spaced between pauses. David's responses were loud and had to be repeated.

'Hullo, Billy.'

'Sorry to be a nuisance.'

'You're not a nuisance.'

'Body going before my brain, thank God!'

'Yes – that's lucky, at least.'

'You're a good chap.'

'Not good enough.'

'I wasn't good enough to my Marie' – Billy had called his wife by the abbreviation of Marigold. 'Look after Emily!'

'I'll try.'

'Any news of Gwen?'

'No – and none from her.'

'Still in Peru?'

'Apparently.'

'With that bloody man?'

'God knows.'

'Gwen's a beautiful person.'

'Yes.'

'She'll come round.'

'We're hoping so. We can't interfere.'

'No. My daugther Jane takes after her mother's family, some of them were wild cats.'

'Are you tired, Billy?'

'Jane was here yesterday.'

'Yes. She's staying with us.'

'That's a pity.'

'Are you tired?'

'Silly to be tired in a hospice.'

'You're not silly.'

'Thanks for coming.'

'No – thank you.'

'Rely on you...'

His eyes closed and his head wobbled. But Emily arrived and woke him.

'You can't be comfortable like that, Father – let me rearrange your pillows,' she called out.

'I've got sleeping sickness,' Billy said.

'Well – you have a sleep – I'll sit with you.'

'What about David?'

'He'll wait or walk home – he'll be fine – won't you, David?'

Billy said: 'Everyone kind...' and again he shut his eyes.

Emily led David to the door of the room.

'You mustn't wait for me, I may spend an hour or even two here,' she said.

'I don't mind how long you are.'

'No, darling...'

'Yes. I'll catch the last of the light in the garden.'

'Did you talk together?'

'Yes.'

'He's so lucid.'

'Yes.'

'He's not in pain – they've given him stuff – it makes him sleepy.'

'How bad is he?'

'They say he might be having a remission.'

'We shouldn't have gone away. I wish we hadn't gone. I didn't know he was in danger.'

'No one knew. Cancers aren't accountable. He wanted us to have a holiday.'

'Will you be okay alone with him? I'll be nearby.'

'I'd like to have him to myself.'

'Don't hurry.'

'Thank you, David.'

Her eyes glistened. He felt his own eyes glistening. He turned away and walked along passages and out of the building.

The garden of St Christopher's was large, with lawns, bushes, trees and paths, and seats for the patients in the warmer summer weather. Now the sun was setting rosily behind the trees, and the dewy lawns seemed to twinkle in the half-light. David had not felt like crying until Emily nearly did, and then he followed suit not really because of Billy's fate – for Billy was old in years, and not tragic – but because he and she were moved for such different reasons. She sorrowed, he was penitent. Her sorrow was genuine, he was sad to have become a fraud. He was no longer what Billy thought and said he was, and he could not compensate his wife for his unfaithfulness by now marking time for her convenience.

He made resolutions. He was definitely not playing the part of Don Jose. Carmen was in another world and he had come down to earth in this one. Rome was over. He aspired to merit Billy's faith in him. If he should ever be faced with a showdown concerning an afternoon in the *Albergo Diurno*, he would tell the truth and pray for pardon. The penalty fitting his crime could be pronounced by Dr Yonak; but, after all, there were ways to disappear before he had injured anybody.

David was in the waiting room when Emily appeared and they walked to their car.

She sat in the passenger seat looking straight ahead, he got into the driver's seat, and, before turning on the ignition, broke the silence between them by asking: 'Was it very difficult for you?'

She replied: 'He's worse. I sensed it. Didn't you?'

'He was sweet to me – he always was.'

'Oh well – it's no use worrying – can we go home?'

He felt sorry, he began to feel sorry for Emily. It was the first emotion of a sympathetic nature she had inspired since their reunion – it was not self-centred. Carmen was eclipsed by the history of his twenty-five years of marriage. He had many more important things than Carmen to deal with.

At Manor Crescent Emily had a question to ask.

'Will we tell Gwen?'

The four words were not a bolt from the blue. For three years they had longed to tell Gwen things and ask her questions, David in particular had longed to do so. But for David who kept no secrets from his daughter, who had confided in her as she had confided in him, Gwen might upset applecarts in the plural. Would she insist on discovering what had happened in Rome? Would she be shocked to find out that her father had behaved almost as foolishly as she had? Would Emily scold her?

'I don't know,' he replied.

'She should be informed.'

'We could be jumping the gun.'

'It's up to you, David.'

'I'm thinking.'

'Jane knows how to contact her.'

'That's part of the problem – she's such a mischief-maker.'

Gwen Crisp had grown up to be the imperfect

element in the story of her so-called perfect parents. She was a remarkable child, never actually beautiful, but intelligent, charming, and shedding radiance on all and sundry. Of course she was romantic, and innocent into the bargain. Aged nineteen she had run off with Hugh Traviss, or he had run off with her – he was forty, married, and his wife Mary had borne him four children. Gwen left a note on the kitchen table for David and Emily. It ran: 'Forgive me, forget me until ... G.' Some months later they received a letter from Lima in Peru – no address on it, the stamps and the franking told the tale. Briefly it asked to be allowed privacy and time to sort out her affair, her affairs, and to right wrongs if she could.

Her family had a bad time of it publicly. The Travisses' home was in Richmond: local feelings ran high against the seduced or the seductress, and her mother and father. Mary Traviss screamed at Emily in the supermarket; business at Macer and Crisp became sluggish; Archie was short of work. David, notwithstanding his and Emily's heartache, stood firm against all the demands for parental action, official investigation, diplomatic assistance – his line was, 'Leave her be, let her work out her own salvation.'

After a few months Mary Traviss and her children decamped, left their home, which was up for sale by an estate agency that was not Macer and Crisp, and were said to be on their way to be reunited with Hugh in Australia. Where did that leave Gwen? Why did she not come home? In time a card arrived again from Lima. She sent loving messages and explained: 'Alone now, but loose ends to tie up.'

Not the least disagreeable aspect of Jane's invasion of her sister's territory was that she had been in Peru, in Lima, in the course of her travels and had met with Gwen, her niece. She brought the news that Gwen was well, and aired her opinion that David and Emily were at fault, were far too strict, were quite inhuman, not to have flown out to South America and rescued the girl, forcibly if necessary. The consequence had been another row. David took exception to her advice, Emily, as usual, to her bossiness.

That had happened about a year after Gwen's elopement. Jane had not been back in Five Oaks between then and her present visitation. For her host and hostess, the parents who had been accused of maltreating their beloved daughter, to have to ask Jane for any favours, let alone how to contact Gwen or even to contact Gwen on their behalf, would be a poisonous pill to swallow. And the mere idea of Jane being the link between Gwen and Billy Williams was offensive to Emily.

In short, the unspoken answer to Emily's queries, 'Will we inform Gwen via Jane?' and 'It's up to you, David,' was 'No, never!'

The Saturday of the week in question came and went without more drama. Billy was no worse, Jane left Manor Crescent early, bound for the bright lights of London where she said she was job-seeking, and returned after the Crisps were in bed. David continued to be amazed that

Emily did not seem to notice that he might be on the verge of a breakdown – she did not even refer to his excuse for keeping his distance.

Sunday meant the Archies for lunch, Archie Crisp, Susan, his wife, and Anna – no Jane, off to London again, luckily. David got to Communion at St Anne's, then had to do last-minute shopping, polish the dining-room table and silver, lay out glass, cutlery, side-plates and napkins, air the wine, make a wood fire in the sitting-room, bring in the high chair for Anna, and stay ahead of the washing-up of saucepans. Emily was always keen to pull out stops for Archie and put on a better show than his wife could.

He was not averse to being kept too busy to brood on other things. He was gladder than usual to be entertaining Archie. His son's development had been successful in all respects except in the avoidance of complacence and pomposity. Archie, the solicitor, had married Susan Witherspoon, a bureaucrat in the Council Offices, a blonde with private means. They were successful together. But Susan when pregnant and then maternal had seemed to get on top of Archie in the moral sense. Just as Emily had smoothed the rough edges of David, so her daughter-in-law house-trained her son.

The luncheon started quite well. Archie was sent home to fetch a special cushion that would make Anna comfortable in the high chair, but he did not complain. Susan twittered amiably and Anna was not sick. David carved the joint of pork, which Archie called 'roast pig', and served the wine when the others were seated at the table. In between Anna's shouts and screams, they talked of Rome, Granpa Billy, Jane, Gwen, and the Archies' ambition to buy a newbuild in Richmond. Archie did most of the talking, while his parents prepared his second helping, picked up his daughter's eating utensils, laughed at his pleasantries and waited for his next brick to drop. He asked if his father was going to be a rat-catcher, R.C. or Roman Catholic, for example; and he said he could afford to buy a better house than the one he lived in, which was the same in all respects as 12 Manor Crescent. However, the mood of the meeting was benign, and for David and seemingly for Emily, the noise and the company eased tension.

After the pork and before the apple crumble, the telephone rang. David went into the sitting-room to take the call.

'Hullo?' he said.

'Mr Crisp?'

'Speaking.'

'I'm the head nurse at St Christopher's Hospice.'

'Is it about my father-in-law?'

'Yes – sad news.'

'Is he dead?'

'He died an hour ago, in his sleep, not stirring at all, he just passed over in his afternoon nap.'

'I'll tell my wife and my family. We're together here.'

'Please feel free to come to the hospice. I'll help you in any way I can. My name's Jo.'

'Thank you, Jo. Thank you. Goodbye.'

'Goodbye, Mr Crisp.'

He was appalled. He had forgotten Billy at probably the moment Billy was dying. They had all forgotten him. But David was especially appalled by himself: he had linked Billy's death with Carmen's. And he had wondered who would be the third to die – deaths often happen in triplicate. He could not control his reactions. He felt accursed. He made a mental and physical effort, stood up, squared his shoulders, re-entered the dining-room and broke the news in a voice that cracked although he was not overcome by sorrow.

Emily cried. He walked round the table to embrace her. Archie was standing, so was Susan, and Anna began to bawl.

David said: 'You should take Anna home.'

Archie said: 'Susan can take her. I'll stay with you and do some organising.'

'No, Archie, you go too – I'll ring you when we need organisation.'

'I meant to make myself useful.'

'Another time, Archie – thanks all the same.'

'Oh very well.'

They returned to the hospice. David supported Emily as she listened to the accounts of nurses. Soon her common sense convinced her that her father had died at the right time, before he was older and iller, and in the right way, peacefully.

So the routine of 'organising' the mundane rites of passage began. Dr Tomkins signed the death certificate. David and Archie registered the death. Jane was taken to see her father for the last time, and allowed to try to convey David and Emily's message by e-mail to Gwen. David engaged funeral directors, Bowden and Sons in Five Oaks High Street, chose the coffin, established that there would be a church service and a second service at the crematorium, reminded Malcolm Bowden that Billy's ashes were to be interred together with those of his wife Marigold, made deals about prices for bearers, transport, available dates, and paid a deposit. Archie saw to the insertion of an announcement of the demise in *The Times, Telegraph* and *Five Oaks Express*: and he and Emily joined David to discuss the funeral in detail with Sam Wilcomb, the Vicar of St Anne's and their friend. Heads were then put together – knocked together largely because of Jane – in order to agree the Order of Service, hymns, readings. Archie undertook the printing of the Order, obtained quotes from printers and so on. Emily with Jane and Susan arranged the floral tributes. David spoke to the organist and the caterers, who would provide sandwiches, cakes, wine and soft drinks for the wake to be held in 12 Manor Crescent: furniture would have to be rearranged to make room for it. Combined with these activities were the lists of the people who needed to be informed personally, of those who would have to have reserved seats in the church, of who would and would not be going from the church to the crem, and of who could sit near whom and who could not be seated near almost anybody. They had to think of ushers, wheelchairs, the choir, of the security of their home while it was occupied exclusively by catering staff. And they all had to answer the telephone calls.

David could not shut up shop for the days of the week following the death of Billy. He served there for snatched mornings and afternoons by agreement with his colleagues. On the Friday afternoon he entered the premises of Macer and Crisp and shut himself into his private office in order to read the business records and correspondence piled on his desk. He had a little 'free' time, that is, time to catch up on work, and he believed that everything possible was made ready for the funeral on the next Monday at midday. He could think of nothing left undone. But time was limited nonetheless, for this was the afternoon on which he was due to meet Dr Yonak and be told the results of his tests. His relief on the one hand was shot through with apprehensiveness on the other. The fears that had been temporarily scattered by duties flocked back into his whole being like homing pigeons.

He tried to concentrate on pages of figures, numbers, letters to be answered, decisions to be taken. He came to a fax, it read: 'So sad for all of you. Struggling to be home in time for Granpa's funeral. Anyway, home for good. At last at last at last. Darling Mum xxx and x for you too, Dad.' He read it again, he read it more closely, and his downtrodden heart lifted up. He prepared to leave the office more bravely than he had entered it. Gwen had given him the courage to accept the sentence about to be delivered by Dr Yonak. He pleaded an emergency with his colleagues, hurried to Five Oaks station and into a London train. At Waterloo he took a Northern Line train to Camden Town.

His thoughts were nearly optimistic for a change. Rome was long ago. Was his nightmare playing itself out? Sex with Emily, or rather no sex, had not been problematical while she mourned. After the funeral, the life and love he was used to could be the order of his days.

The tests were negative – nothing was wrong.

He thanked God. As a thanks offering, he had the idea of visiting his parents. He took a taxi across North London to Maida Vale. David's father and mother were tearful to see their son again, he too shed tears for one reason and another. He told them about Billy, he attempted to fill gaps, and promised to communicate in the next few weeks. But he had to leave them, he could not desert Emily, he would have to explain why he was being absent for so long.

He hailed another taxi, was pleased to spend celebratory money, and asked the driver to take him to Victoria Station via Regent's Park and Hyde Park. He wanted to see those parks, known since his childhood – it would be a sort of treat for him, and the underground would get him across from Victoria to Waterloo. He studied the trees that had grown up, the autumn colours of leaves, and imagined the greens of spring.

The taxi was held up in Park Lane. Traffic jammed outside the Dorchester Hotel, and David gazed through a window at the uniformed commissionaire opening the passenger door of a chauffeur-driven car. A gentleman stepped out and offered a hand to a lady. She emerged, and she was Carmen.

CHAPTER FIVE

David asked: 'What happened?'

He was in an uncomfortable position, lying down with his legs bent double. Men were looking at him, two or three men in yellow coats, and he looked up at them.

'You flaked out, mate,' somebody said.

'Relax, sir – we're going to move you,' another man said.

'Where am I?'

'You're on the floor of my taxi, that's where.'

His legs were being pulled, literally, and at the same time strong arms were lifting and dragging him in the opposite direction.

'What are you doing?'

'It's the police, mate, they're trying to get you out.'

His head lolled and banged against a hard object, and he recovered some of his senses.

'Did I faint?'

'That's it.'

'I can help myself now.'

He was in the fresh air, trying to stand on grass, being supported by two people in the yellow coats, while traffic whooshed past.

'Where are we?'

'Hyde Park Corner, we're in the Park. There'll be a police vehicle along in a minute. Are you ill, sir?'

'No, I just fainted, I had a shock.'

'We'll see if you need an ambulance. No bones broken, are there?'

'No, no, nothing like that. Thank you for helping me. I'll have to go home.'

The man not in yellow spoke: 'Pardon me, there's my fare to settle. You're owing money, sir.'

'Oh yes – sorry – how much do I owe?'

'With the wait, twelve pound.'

David hauled his wallet out of a hip pocket, extracted a twenty pound note, studied it for a moment, struggling with sums, then asked for a fiver.

'That'll do nicely. You wouldn't be wanting a taxi home? Where do you live?'

'Five Oaks, near Richmond.'

'Too far for me, sorry.'

'I'll be going by public transport anyway.'

'Okay, all the best, ta-ta.'

The taxi drove off. The yellow coats were worn by a policeman and a policewoman. David was standing with them by their car – leaning against it. The policewoman was explaining that they were a police patrol, they had to carry on with their work, the officers who would be taking charge of the incident were from the Special Duties Department.

Another vehicle arrived, a people-carrier; two more police, again a man and a woman, stepped out and greeted everyone. They assisted David into a back seat and the woman began to ask questions and write on a clip-board – the other police had gone when he looked for them.

He said: 'I'm perfectly able to look after myself now. Thank you, but I really want to be on my way.'

They had to take details, it was the law, they said.

David foresaw a thousand complications and tried to open the door he sat beside – it would not open.

He protested in vain. If he managed to run away, they said they would have to arrest him. They were law-abiding to a fault, and in the end he surrendered and cooperated. He let them drive him to Five Oaks, he seemed to have no alternative, and shut his eyes and prayed that Emily might be out when they reached Manor Crescent.

She was in. Both police officers insisted on escorting him to his front door and on ringing his doorbell although he showed them his latchkey. Emily opened the door and gasped. At least the policeman had the grace to say that no offence had been committed, but he then gave an account of the episode.

'Thank you and goodbye,' David eventually said and slammed the door.

Emily supported him into the sitting-room.

'I'm fine,' he assured her, laughing. 'It's a storm in a teacup. I fainted briefly – don't know why.'

'What was the shock?'

'Shock? I don't know. Exhaustion, I expect – we're all pretty tired, aren't we? – and I'd been to see my people.'

'Your parents? You've been there?'

'I agree it's surprising. I went to call on them on the spur of the moment, and our time together was emotional – it kind of knocked me on the head, I suppose.'

'David, are you ill?'

'Not at all, not that I know of.'

'But your waterworks?'

'Normal again – I meant to tell you.'

'What was all that about, the infection?'

'I wasn't taking risks, I didn't want to infect you, and I was right – it would have been awful for you to have cystitis or something during the funeral.'

'It's bad enough to have you fainting and being brought home in a police car – I could have done without that.'

'I'm sorry. I couldn't help it, I didn't faint on purpose.'

'No, darling, no – poor you! Are you really better? Do you want a cup of tea or a drink?'

'I might go and lie down for ten minutes.'

'Can I get you anything, an aspirin or a hot water bottle?'

They laughed. She was standing, he sat on a chair, looking up at her – or nearly at her. She reached out an arm, he took her hand, she pulled him to his feet, hugged him and kissed him on the lips. He disentangled himself.

'Oh – I forgot – Gwen's coming home.'

'What?'

'She sent us a fax to the office. She's heading home.'

'When, David?'

'No details – lots of kisses for you – one for me – she's trying to be here in time for Granpa – Jane must have been in touch with her.'

'Oh that's marvellous!'

'Home for good, she says.'

'Oh David!'

'Perhaps that was the shock for me. I rang you as soon as I got the fax, but you were out, and I had to hurry to be in Maida Vale where I was expected.'

'Will she tell us why she stayed away so long?'

'Maybe, maybe not. We'd better wait and see. We've been so careful not to be inquisitive or possessive. Sorry – I don't seem to know much today.'

'No – of course – you go and rest – you do look wan. I'll ring Doctor Tomkins if you feel any worse.'

'Thank you, darling.'

He climbed the stairs, and in their bedroom sat on the edge of his bed, then leant forwards and covered his eyes with his hands. He was hoping and trying not to faint again.

It was all too much for him. He had not been sure whether to be pleased with or afraid of the police. He felt cut up inside by lying, lying to Emily. And he had seen the ghost of Carmen.

He shook all over. Was she a ghost, or the flesh and blood he remembered? She had been dead and was alive – ghosts are not ushered out of luxury cars and into the Dorchester Hotel in time for cocktails. It was not supernatural, nor reasonable, nor likely. She had lain on the bed in the *Albergo Diurno* while he was in the washroom in the position in which she wished him to make more love to her. She had not lain so in order to die – on the contrary – she had died in spite of awaiting the payment of a further compliment from her lover. No! He rejected the proof of his eyes. He was mistaken. He salvaged memories that he had banished to the depths of his consciousness. He had never expected to want to think about Carmen again, had felt it would be tempting providence to entertain such thoughts. But now the picture of a woman with long dark curly hair, questing eyes, inviting lips, challenging teeth, flashed up for comparison with the other woman at the Dorchester. But the latter was smart, the former had worn gipsy-like layers of brightly coloured garments soon to be discarded; the latter had brown hair gathered up neatly; she had dignity, not flexuous movements and animal grace. They were not the same. They could not be.

Who was she with this evening? Memory jogged his elbow, it would not allow him to wriggle out of disagreeable details. His partner in crime was married, she had worn a wedding ring as he did, and played a silent little game with their rings by way of overture to the vows and laws they were about to break. He again saw them on the table, his and hers, symbols of their promises never to do what was about to be done. How painful it was to recall the excitement of the novelty of sin!

Another question sprang to mind: who had she been betraying? Was it the man who offered her his hand as she emerged from the car, a tall senior citizen, a stuffed shirt? He – that old boy – would never be able to satisfy Carmen, David argued inwardly. A scenario that made some sense presented itself to him. Carmen was married to a husband who could afford to lap her in luxury but was impotent. She therefore impersonated the heroine of a raunchy book and fornicated with a stranger in seedy premises. Where did death fit in? Where did life after death? He was nonplussed.

He stretched out horizontally on his bed. Carmen in the book is murdered by her lover. She has driven him to kill and no doubt to die. Neither of those things had happened. But, in reality, and possibly, Carmen lived to seek him out and cause more havoc. No, he groaned. He could see no light at the end of his tunnel, and was tempted by images of high bridges over fast-flowing rivers or a bottle of sleeping pills.

He must have been dozing. He awoke with a start and Emily's name on his lips. He loved her. And they had a roof over their heads, their daughter would soon be with them, their son was really a good boy, they had a grandchild, and health and, by many standards, wealth – perhaps he was compounding his sin by repining and dreaming of suicide.

The question remained: would Emily ever see it that way?

The telephone rang. She answered it. He should be helping her. He hurried downstairs.

The rest of the day passed, they got through it. Emily was overworked and overwrought. The reason why the telephone had not rung for most of the time he was 'resting' was because she was speaking on it. She said she had had to talk to a dozen of Billy's old friends who were fussing about the funeral. Now, she was having to answer calls from women wanting to know if they should wear hats for the service.

In between she expressed concern for David's health somewhat brusquely: 'Oh dear oh dear, what is the matter with you? ... You don't seem to be yourself ... Am I to get the doctor to you before or after the funeral? ... Will you stand up to the next three days?'

He said he would. His apologies seemed to displease. She was not interested in supper, he cooked himself a fried egg and baked beans and ate an apple and took one telephone call. It was from Jane, saying she had decided to stay in London for a bit as funerals were bad for her nerves. He looked at the news on TV and returned to his bed before she was ready for hers.

On Saturday he ran errands. He was shopping for food, then accompanying Archie to the printers of the Order of Service leaflets and fighting for the correction of errors. He was brushing his black suit and finding his black tie. On Sunday it was church and confabulation with Sam Wilcomb, with the organist and members of the choir, with ushers, and a long session with the florists. Archie confused issues, Susan brought Anna along to help and hinder, and Gwen did not arrive.

For David, the contrasts between the social ritual, his emotional turmoil, and the death of Billy, affected him like dazzling lights.

On Monday morning, in the Crisps' bedroom, first thing in the early morning, Emily asked David: 'Are you up to all that's going to happen today?'

'I am. Are you?'

'I hope so, and hoping it's not going to be bad for you.'

'How can you think of me when you've many more important things to think about?'

'Nothing more important...'

'Oh Emily, I wish I deserved you!'

'What do you mean?'

'You're so unselfish.'

'I love you. Do you love me?'

'Yes, of course! Of course I do.'

'Thank you.'

'No, no – it's the other way round.'

The rush began: worries multiplying, telephone calls, breakfast, last minute amendments, dressing, studying weather, arrival of Archie and Susan – Anna was coming to the wake – arrival of David's parents in their unaccustomed clothes smelling of mothballs, and the black minibus driven by Malcolm Bowden waiting in the roadway. David

79

postponed departure for the sake of Gwen, but no sign of her – the family climbed into the bus and processed slowly the few hundred yards to the church. It was full to overflowing. There were the friends of the Crisps, of Billy and Marigold, nurses from the Hospice, colleagues of Emily and David and Archie, the Tomkinses, neighbours, God knew who else. The coffin was in position before the altar. Joe Macer, one of the ushers, led the way to the front pew. Sam Wilcomb without surplice was fiddling with books in the pulpit. Organ musak and hushed chatter was the background to David's anxiety and suspicion that he might fail everyone somehow or other.

Silence fell. The choir filed in, four or five greybeards, four plump girls, all in white surplices. Sam in a different sort of vestment, brightly coloured, modern design, entered and faced the congregation. He made some introductory remarks, referring to Billy, standing close to the coffin and gesturing at it as if to slap Billy on the back, and announced the hymn to be sung, *Abide with me.*

David's reading was next. He was to read from Chapter 13 of St Paul's First Epistle to the Corinthians, beginning: 'Though I speak with the tongues of men and of angels, and have not charity...' At least, that was what he had expected to read; but when he looked at the page in the New Bible on the lectern in St Anne's he saw that the word 'charity' was replaced with the word 'love'. The exchange was for the worse in

80

his opinion. It altered the sense and rhythm of the sentences. And for personal reasons he wished he could have reverted to the older form; but it was too late to make difficulties. He thought belatedly that he should have asked Archie to spare him the imminent ordeal.

He began well. But halfway through a door creaked at the back of the church, he raised his eyes and saw over the heads of the congregation somebody coming in, a woman, a woman whose eyes met his, who smiled and waved – Gwen. He looked again at the text, and stuttered. Instead of a description of charity, he saw words that were unreadable and unspeakable. He was not a hypocrite, he had no right to preach about love. Gwen had pushed him over an edge, his sight as well as his speech failed him, he was holding on to the sides of the lectern, and Sam Wilcomb was keeping him on his feet and leading him back to his seat beside Emily. She had her arm round his neck, and he wanted to die.

He sat with his head not far from his knees. He seemed to be made of embarrassment and misery. Emily stroked his back and then leant down to ask him questions in a tearful whisper.

'Do you want to get out of the church?'

'No.'

'Are you ill?'

'No.'

'Don't worry, darling.'

'Sorry, sorry!'

'Don't come out at the end of the service.'

'No.'

'Stay where you are. Archie'll look after you.'

'Oh dear!'

'Poor David!'

He stood for the last hymn and the blessing – the address by General Lumsdown, Billy's old comrade-in-arms and friend, and the prayers, did not reach into David's private hell. The undertakers trooped up the aisle and lifted the coffin on to their shoulders.

'Do stay here,' Emily whispered.

But he shook his head, linked her arm in his, and they walked towards the open door, where Gwen waited. He and Gwen embraced, then Emily and Gwen did so, and all three shed tears. Out of doors, while the coffin was loaded into the hearse, in a snatch of conversation, it was arranged that Gwen would come down from London to Manor Crescent for lunch on the next day. David and Archie stepped into another car and were driven to say farewell to Billy in the Crematorium.

For some hours David had moments of envying his father-in-law. At the wake he was subjected to interrogation and varying degrees of torture by concerned persons. Gwen had not stayed in Five Oaks to socialise with strangers.

She spoke to her parents on the telephone that evening – it was a 'conference call', the upstairs telephone at Manor Crescent was used as well as the downstairs one. Yes, David assured her in answer to her first question, he had recovered, he had just been sad; and Emily chimed in to say she was under the impression she had survived – no, seriously, she was relieved it was all over. Then Gwen began to answer their questions. Yes, she too was okay, more than okay, never better. She was staying in London because she had not wanted to disrupt the funeral, and she had not been sure of the reception she would get in Five Oaks – she meant from people other than her family. She thanked them repeatedly for having always 'been there for her', for not judging or condemning her, for not butting in even though they did not know her whys and wherefores, and for the warmth of her welcome. Why three years, why so terribly long, why had she almost buried herself in Lima, and why had she shut everyone out? She answered briefly. She would explain more when she was at home again. She had been repaying the debts Hugh Traviss had run up; she had not been able to explain all in a letter or an expensive call; and she was afraid of involving her parents in the trouble she had got herself into and simply had to get herself out of.

She finished the conversation then – she had an engagement. They all postponed it reluctantly. David and Emily ran the gamut of predictable emotions – between the grief of bereavement and the joy of reunion – between that ending and the beginning on the next day.

At Manor Crescent the three of them had a chance to look at one another more closely than had been possible in the crush outside St Anne's. Gwen paid her parents compliments, Emily returned them, and David found his daughter at once the same and different. The vivid personality was unchanged, and the outgoing sweetness; but she was no longer a girl with heavy hair the wrong length and dowdy clothes. She was a slim smart woman. They took up where they had left off the previous evening.

'Are you better today, Dad?'

'Better for seeing you.'

'You were devoted to Granpa, weren't you?'

'Yes, that was it.'

'And Mum, poor Mum, you'll miss him so.'

'Yes, but ... I'm not alone, thank goodness. Am I right or wrong to think you were alone for most of the time in South America?'

'Right – Hugh left me three months after we landed there.'

Exclamations of one sort and another boiled down to the question of the debts.

'He booked us into a grand hotel and bought me clothes and presents.'

'Did he pay for nothing?'

'He had no money. He lived on plastic, on tick. His wife, Mary, had the family money.'

'Was Mary's money what he left you for?'

'Roughly speaking, yes.'

'How were you expected to manage with a pile of debts in a foreign country – how were you meant to eat, how were you to get back to England?'

'He only pities himself. His thought was that you and Dad would "cough up", as he put it, which was exactly what I wouldn't allow to happen.'

Why, Emily asked, she could not help asking, why had Gwen done it? The unspoken part of the question was: stolen another woman's husband and the father of four children, flown in the face of morality and the conventions, shamed her parents, shocked and worried everyone?

'All I can say is,' Gwen replied, 'that innocence is more innocent than experienced people imagine. Hugh's sales pitch is pathos. His father died young, he was an only child and his mother spoilt him. He was professionally hopeless. I was one of quite a few women who bought his tale of woe.'

'Were you ever happy?' Emily persisted.

'For a night or two.'

'You're lucky not to have had a baby.'

'Wasn't that clueless, Mum, and I learnt a lot in record time.'

'Well, he's not here – you won't have to meet him. You'll have to make a fresh start.'

'Oh Mum ... How I wish ... I did such a bad thing...'

'But you paid your debts – it was very honest of you, and must have been very difficult. Was it a large sum?'

'Thousands.'

'Goodness me!'

'I got a good job and lived on a quarter of my salary. Paying back the money was the easy bit.'

'It's over, darling,' Emily said. 'You've saved your soul. You've corrected your mistake. I admire you. Anyway, you're here with us. I feel like celebrating. Can we, David?'

David opened a bottle of champagne, but his hands were shaking too much for him to pour it out – he left the task to Gwen. Gradually he controlled his yearning to seek his own salvation there and then, confess and hope to be absolved, tell his daughter there was another bond between them, and hug and kiss her, expressing his sympathy and perhaps winning hers. The talk took a less personal turn, and Aunt Jane was discussed and disapproved of, and the Archies were analysed with indulgence. Gwen wanted news of her Crisp grandparents and to visit them soon. Her plan for the future was already under way. She had paid the deposit on a bachelor flat in Pimlico – yes, she had money saved for the expenses of independence; and she had the offer of a job in a branch of the bank that had employed her in Lima. And she was meeting the representative of another bank at five o'clock that very afternoon – she might receive an improved offer.

Mother and daughter made their long-drawn-out *au revoirs*, and David walked with Gwen to Five Oaks station.

Each tried to make loving declarations to the other.

Then, after a few preliminaries, David said his prepared piece: 'You've done the impossible – you seem to have turned the millstone round your neck into the foundation of a new life.'

'What a funny way of putting it! But thanks, Dad.'

'Love can work miracles, too – we must remember that.'

'It's all right, I'm all right – don't worry.'

'Is there a knight in shining armour?'

'Not really. My eye's in now. I can spot a cad from a long distance. No more free gifts – why have girls forgotten love's a bargain or it's not worth having?'

'Ask me another!'

'Oh Dad, thank you for having your feet on the ground.'

'Don't be too sure of me, Gwen.'

'Why not?'

'We all have feet of clay. Your destiny's your business and no one else's.'

'But you'll help me, won't you? You'll tell me when I'm asking for trouble.'

'I should ask you.'

'What?'

'Nothing.'

'Find me a nice man who'll give me children and be kind to us and won't object to a quiet life!'

'That's ... That's such a good idea. Dear girl, we're nearly at the station. Can you give me your telephone number? We'll ring to suggest another visit, or you could ring – Mum would like you to ring her. And you've got my office number, haven't you?'

'I have. Goodbye, Dad. Take care, won't you?'

'Everyone says "Take care" nowadays.'

'I mean, see a good doctor if anything's wrong.'

'Yes, yes.'

They parted. He looked back at her and she looked back at him, and they smiled at each other and waved.

As he walked on towards the office the rush of events of the last few days, the days of diversion, even his crisis at the funeral, all faded into insignificance, and he was confronted by the memory of having either seen the ghost of Carmen or Carmen very much alive.

He could not forget it. He had failed to forget. He was outside Bowden's the undertakers: to be there at that moment struck him as a coincidental hint he had to take. He entered the shop and asked to see Mr Malcolm Bowden.

They shook hands. They were fellow shopkeepers and old acquaintances. Malcolm asked David if the funerary arrangements were satisfactory, and David replied that they could not have been better.

David drew him aside and asked a question in an undertone.

'Malcolm, could you settle an argument I've been having with a friend? Am I right to think and say that if you're dead you're dead, and, barring miracles, that's the end of the story?'

'It depends.'

'Depends? My friend has argued something of the sort. Depends on what?'

'We have to make very sure before we seal a coffin.'

'But a person must be certified to have died, a corpse must be transferred to a morgue, isn't that so?'

'Oversights have occurred. We are constantly warned by the regulator of our trade to check still further.'

'Check how and for what?'

'For suspended animation. Its medical name is catalepsy.'

CHAPTER SIX

David Crisp thanked Malcolm Bowden for the information and walked out into the fresh air, of which he inhaled deep breaths. He had been in an undertaker's premises and thought that he might as well have stayed there. Carmen had not necessarily died in the *Albergo Diurno*, she could be alive, she could have entered the Dorchester Hotel the other day, and she might take it into her head to pay him a visit and put the ultimate kibosh on his life.

What a hell of a mistake! And of a woman! Carmen was responsible for a sexual fiesta, and regrets, guilt, sickness, fear – now he was racked by a mixture of almost superstitious awe and incipient anger. He foresaw a future of jumping out of his skin when the telephone or the doorbell rang, of scenes with Carmen, of rows with Emily, who in her whole-hearted way might reject him utterly and, broken-hearted, evict him from the marital home.

He was more than stunned – if possible – by Malcolm's answer. He had expected a categorical endorsement of 'dead' meaning 'dead'. He had been too startled to ask for a definition of catalepsy. He departed with a dangerous word repeating itself in his head instead of a memorial hallelujah. He could not face his colleagues in the office, let alone Emily. He was near the library, saw its door was open and walked in. A man at a desk looked up from his computer screen and asked a question.

'Oh – thank you – yes – I need information,' David replied.

'What kind of information?'

'Medical.'

'Do you want to be directed to our medical section?'

'Maybe.'

'Can you be more definite, sir?'

'Do you have an *Encyclopaedia Britannica*?'

'Yes, on the first floor, next to General Medical.'

'Thank you.'

He mounted stairs, found the relevant volume, and read that catalepsy is a trance-like state of suspended animation, loss of voluntary motion, and probably caused by hysteria or schizophrenia.

He saw a medical dictionary, but did not dare to open it. He was afraid it would tell him that catalepsy is not a mortal disease, and that, although pretty well indistinguishable from death, patients soon recover health and strength. The peculiarities of his adultery were piling up. Carmen's fierce embraces in a basement room with flies thrown in were not lust but pathology, she had chosen him not for his good looks but because she was hysterical and desirous of having any stray man between her legs. He did not want to read analyses of red-hot lust written by a scientist. Besides, he had another idea.

He left the library and in his sanctum at Macer and Crisp he rang a telephone number.

'Max,' he said.

'Is it my friend in the sticks?'

'It's David.'

'I thought as much.'

'Can you talk? Are you alone?'

'Fire ahead!'

'Actually I'd like to talk somewhere else. Could you lunch with me tomorrow? I'll come to London – it's Emily's day at St Christopher's Hospice.'

'God, she's good! Okay, a quickie.'

They fixed to meet in a pub, The Goat and Compasses, off Stamford Street near Waterloo, and convenient for both.

David worked for the remainder of the afternoon, gritted his teeth and returned to Manor Crescent. But the evening passed anti-climactically. They talked about Gwen. Then Emily answered letters of condolence from friends of her father, and at an early hour she said he was still looking peaky and packed him off to bed.

At The Goat and Compasses the next day David and Max Harrison met, ordered food and drink, and sat down in a quiet corner.

'What's the score?' Max asked, and corrected himself with a giggle: 'I've used a tactless word, haven't I? Sorry! What's the damage? That sounds better.'

David described his extra-marital experience in Rome.

'Crikey!' Max commented.

'It doesn't stop there,' David said.

'Hold hard! You mean the lady – well, the woman – passed over in the middle of the action?'

'I was in the washroom and she'd gone when I emerged.'

'Lucky you weren't somewhere else! I've heard of a man who got caught in a most embarrassing position by *rigor mortis* – he couldn't extricate himself for hours.'

'Only you hear about things like that, Max. But I haven't finished.'

'I can't believe you've anything worse to tell me.'

'I've seen her since then.'

'Alive?'

'Walking into the Dorchester.'

'Tell the truth, David!'

'I am. To the best of my knowledge and belief, I saw her getting out of a car and walking into the Dorchester Hotel with a man.'

'You made a mistake in Rome. You could have made another in Hyde Park. Your truth's a bit far-fetched, isn't it?'

'Not necessarily. Have you heard of catalepsy?'

'If it's a sexual disease, I'm surprised to say that I don't think I have. Incidentally, did our doctor give you a clear bill?'

'Oh yes – I should have told you – yes, thanks. But catalepsy, Max, it's a disease all right, but not sexual. It's death in life. You can have a cataleptic stroke. You can find yourself in the morgue. Alternatively, you can find yourself, if nobody finds out that you're alive, being buried or cremated.'

'By golly, yes – I've had a second thought –

it happened to the man who wrote *Manon Lescaut*. Are you with me?'

'A book with that title?'

'Yes – French – they call it a classic – we might call it soft porn – damn good stuff. The author was found to be alive by the undertaker who was lifting him into his coffin. What's the cause of the disease? I suppose you were.'

'I was afraid the police would suppose that, too. But I haven't been accused of a *crime passionel* so far. The disease is apparently a symptom of hysteria or schizophrenia.'

'No wonder the woman was good in bed. She was good, I bet.'

'Why – what are you getting at?'

'Neurotics are great lovers, but they only make love when they're inclined to, which can mean once in a blue moon.'

'Max, that's not helpful – you haven't asked me yet why I arranged this meeting in a hurry.'

'Tell me!'

'Until yesterday afternoon I was convinced she, my partner in crime, was dead and gone, therefore I had nothing to fear from her. But now I've been told that I really could have seen her at the Dorchester, I might not have been seeing a ghost, she could be as large as life, she was in London, and might come after me. I hope I'm flattering myself, yet can't get rid of the idea that she'll confront me and Emily and slit our throats. What do you think?'

'You exaggerate, that's what. Give me a thumbnail sketch of her.'

'A lady, not a common slut – sensitive as well as vicious – purrs like a kitten and can be a tiger – I don't know.'

'Does she know who you are? It's the crux of the matter.'

'I'm afraid I told her the name of my hotel in Rome.'

'So she could trace you?'

'I'm not absolutely sure, but … Yes.'

'You don't want to have another shot at the target by any chance?'

'Good God, no!'

'Don't speak to her on the telephone, don't speak to her on your doorstep, don't answer any letter or note, and if the worst comes to the worst put the police on to a stalker.'

'I haven't got her name.'

'Take the number of her car, try to get her telephone number if she rings up, identify her and complain to her family, don't weaken, David, don't try to play by the Queensberry Rules, because women don't, they play by the laws of the jungle.'

'You're frightening me more than she does.'

'Well, it'll end somehow some time, she's died once, she may do it better next time. Womanisers take their female hurdles in their stride, cheer up!'

'I'm not a womaniser, and I'm not like you, Max.'

'That's a bonus.'

'But I trust you. Am I right to trust you?'

'Spot on!'

That evening, when he arrived home, Emily had news for him. David's heart missed a beat when she said that all sorts of people had rung up; but her smile was reassuring. She had had a lovely talk with Gwen, who landed that job she was hoping for. Then Gloria had rung up – David took a moment to remember that Emily was talking about his mother. Not a crisis, Emily was quick and kind to say: Hector and Gloria had invited all the younger Crisps to their golden wedding tea party on a Sunday afternoon, and they had been so sweet and modest that Emily was determined to make up for having neglected her in-laws. Emily continued: Archie and Susan had both rung. Archie was delighted to hear that Gwen had returned and was going to be a banker. Susan's call had come after Gloria's, Emily was able to tell her about the tea party. Later, Archie and Susan spoke on the same line to say that they would be really pleased to take tea with the grandparents, and hoped Gwen could join in. There had also been a call from Joe Macer: apparently the sale of an expensive property in Richmond had become a done-deal.

In short, the news for David was not bad. He felt the octopus of his family getting a grip of him, which was protective as well as dangerous. His recall to the top priorities pushed Carmen down the list of his preoccupations. Some days passed without anything dire happening. He was off and on aware that he had not been thinking of the damage Carmen could do with her clever little hands. He lost himself in his business in working hours, and when night fell nobody demanded an answer to the sex question. He and Emily both had other matters to lull them to sleep.

He again dared to wonder if his fears boiled down to cowardice. He was guilty, true, but not of murder; he had no need to shrink away from policemen; and why would Carmen think she could hurt him without hurting herself? Carmen would surely be a great embarrassment to the classy lady tittupping into the Dorchester. The gent she was with, her husband, partner or companion, was unlikely to be pleased to discover that she sometimes let down her hair, had it curled, dressed like a Spanish whore, and dragged a stranger into a day-hotel for fun and games nearly to die for.

David looked forward instead of over his shoulder, the reunion of Crisps would be an antidote to the demise of Billy Williams and the orphanhood of Emily. Archie volunteered to drive his parents to North London in his second-hand Mercedes – Gwen would travel by the Victoria and Bakerloo lines from Pimlico to Maida Vale. At about three o'clock they met outside the house in Saturn Street and rang the doorbell. Hector and Gloria opened the door, they trooped in, packed into the parlour, and Emily produced a basketful of presents, a bottle of champagne, flowers, trinkets wrapped in gold paper, and David's cheque in a golden envelope.

Congratulations and thanks were exchanged. Hector spoke up to draw attention to the golden wedding coming so soon after the silver wedding of David and Emily. Susan needed privacy in which to deal with Anna's requirements and was directed to the upstairs bathroom. Emily and Gwen volunteered to help Gloria in the kitchen, to cut sandwiches and move furniture. Hector acceded to his grandson's request for another visit to the shed in the garden, where the work with fine furniture was done – Archie had loved it when he was a boy.

Hector, David and Archie studied the craftsman's traditional tools, the saws of all sizes and chisels that looked like spoons and hatpins, and the modern labour-saving machines. Hector had been mending a chair inlaid with ivory and a desk with fifteen mystery compartments. He explained and gave demonstrations of his expertise.

Then he said: 'I was hoping to have a word about the future, I mean Gloria's and mine. We're in our eighties and have made our wills very simple, only one sheet of paper apiece, but legal. I leave everything to her and she leaves everything to me, and then we both leave what's left to you, David, for onward transmission to Gwen and Archie and Anna, if the taxman permits. Archie, we've named you and your father to be executors – I always have to be careful not to say executioners! We've kept quite healthy, thanks be, but it's best to be prepared. Neither of us wants you to ruin yourselves with paying for our care. We'd like to stay here as long as we can, and then for the survivor to let the NHS cope.

That's mainly what I wanted to tell you. Don't waste all your inheritance on us.'

After suitable responses to this speech, the trio returned to the house and set about the tea, the sandwiches of lettuce with Marmite and ham with mustard, of homemade cakes, one with a cream and strawberry jam filling and another with chocolate cream in the middle, all delicious.

The talk was cheerful, but David smiled in order to hide his sadness. He smiled and laughed until his face ached. He was comparing his parents' marriage with what had happened to his own. He was wishing in vain that he had been and was as true as his father.

After tea the bottle of champagne was opened and they all got enough in the bottoms of wine glasses to drink toasts. When David had thanked his parents for having brought him into the world and for always being good to him, Hector replied that not he but Gloria deserved the compliments, and proposed to divert David's toast in her direction. They duly raised their glasses to Gloria, who was persuaded to say a few words.

'No, no – he's flattering me – don't you believe him – I'm the lucky one. Nice men don't grow on trees, that's a fact. Let's drink his health. Raise your glasses to a gentleman!'

Then Susan said it was Anna's bedtime, and the party broke up.

David resolved again to rise above his circumstances. He would not quail before a woman who seemed to be disputing control of his imagination. He would be more like his father. He thought of doing more for Emily, perhaps taking her on another holiday as soon as she would not probe into his motives.

Days passed without any disaster of the sort he dreaded. Nothing in particular upset the equilibrium he was slowly recovering. He hoped with more conviction that Carmen would never more cross his path. The vibrations at home were less tense – Granpa Billy was in heaven, as Emily told Anna. There was a pleasant weekend in the offing, Gwen was coming to stay, and they were going to lunch with the Archies on Sunday.

In the week before that weekend the so-called 'French Market' was coming to Five Oaks. It was composed of French street-traders who arrived by sea and river and set up their stalls in the High Street – they always came on Wednesday afternoons, which was early closing time for the Five Oaks shops. Wednesday was also a half-day for Macer and Crisp – the staff worked all day on Saturdays. Round about one o'clock on the Wednesday in question the door of the estate agency was locked and Joe and the others took their leave. David stayed behind to complete paperwork and finish his lunchtime sandwich. He finally let himself out into the street barred to traffic and transformed by two lines of stalls selling food and clothing, under brightly coloured canopies, and by a milling crowd in between.

He thought he would buy something for Emily, a surprise. He joined the throng of people buying goods at inflated prices, bread-sticks a metre long, pricey cheeses covered with green mould, novelty pancakes off a griddle, berets and saucy postcards. The noise level was high, the traders shouted, the consumers laughed at them, girls giggled, children screamed. David was amused, and he liked the smell of French cookery. He fell for a scarf and apple fritters – she could give the scarf to a friend for Christmas if it was unsuitable, and they could eat the fritters for supper.

He was near one end of the lines of stalls, sauntering in the direction of Manor Crescent. It was a sunny day, quite warm in the early afternoon for the end of October. A woman inspecting goods in a stall selling trashy jewellery wore smarter clothes than the natives of Five Oaks. She was elegant, too, standing there a short distance ahead of him. And he recognised her.

He was transfixed, rooted to the ground, and felt the blood rushing to his face and his heart thumping. Was he wrong? He could not be right. It was impossible – and so had his life become. Fear took over. He was afraid she would see him. He walked away, strode away, but then stopped. He looked back, she had moved on slowly, he could catch glimpses of her through gaps in the intervening crush. She was by a stall on the other side, on the left, inspecting lengths of material. She turned her head. He turned his, turned the back of his head towards her, and awaited with great trepidation the pressure of her hand on some spot of his anatomy. Nothing happened.

He was imagining, he was over-reacting – she had not seen him, she could not pick him out of a score of shoppers; and there she still was, holding a roll of red satin against the sun. Red satin – Carmen's colour – she had worn a satin scarf – and he felt weak in the knees.

She did not buy the satin, and she strolled on slowly – why was she not in a hurry? What was she doing in Five Oaks? He had jumped to the conclusion that she was where he was on purpose, and now rationalised his reflexes. The Dorchester Hotel and his home town might as well have been on different planets, she could only be in Five Oaks because she had found out that he lived there – she had wheedled his name and address out of the Hotel Universal in Rome. It followed that she had also discovered he was married, he had been staying at the hotel with Mrs Crisp, his wedding ring that she had expertly removed referred to his marriage that was very much in force. Did she intend to break it up? He shuddered to think of Carmen confronting Emily. He was in a sea of the most awful possibilities, and momentarily out of his depth.

But he could not easily get home without passing her, he had to keep watch on her in order to protect Emily, he must shadow her for innumerable reasons, he could not stop himself.

He scanned the scene: no sign of her. He was almost as worried by not seeing her as he had been when he saw her. He dodged in and out of the crowd. She had advanced roughly halfway along the twin lines of stalls, and was buying something from a stall displaying varicoloured sweets in trays and glass bottles – she was buying a paperbagful of sweets. She was not a child, she was an adult with suspect wealth of experience of the darker arts of love, but her purchase was childlike, misleading. She was wearing a skirt and a jacket of suede or something like it, well cut, nipping her waist, partly covering her slightly revealing skirt. She was a smart woman, with her hair up or shortened, and she actually looked fit, even athletic, far from moribund. David noticed men eyeing her, but she was not noticing. She sucked one of her sweets instead.

David shook himself. Carmen was again moving at a leisurely pace through the sunny afternoon and neatly side-stepping the other people. How did she get to Five Oaks, he wondered, how would she leave it? And when? She was not staying in the place, for pity's sake? Was she going to lay siege to himself – and his family?

Another bout of panic washed his emotional slate clean and seemed to write on it: how dare she? He was annoyed, angry, outraged, and on the point of casting discretion aside. He blamed her for everything more than he blamed himself: that was the change in his attitude. She had done him a bad turn in Rome, two, in fact, she had visited upon him adultery and a potential murder charge. She had poisoned his relations with his family. Now she had come back to scare him and, arguably, do worse, much worse.

She had speeded up, she was fifty metres ahead of him, beyond the market stalls, and pausing for a moment by Archer Street, which led into Manor Crescent. He walked quicker – was she looking at the name of the street on a sign because she knew the way to where he lived? But she continued quicker still – he broke into a run, because he was ready to warn her off and give her a piece of his mind. He ran after her, and at the same time a horde of consumers, new would-be shoppers, brought in by rail or buses, advanced towards him in a rowdy mass. He was hindered, could not get through, was held back by people saying, 'Mind out! Do you mind!' He saw Carmen, she was approaching a line of parked cars, she must be going to drive away, and he began to fight, use his elbows, struggle to reach her and punish her. At last he waved at her and called out loud 'Carmen!' But the people closed in, and when he could next get a view of the road a car was manoeuvring out, one of two cars pulling out of Five Oaks.

He was furious. She had escaped correction. He had done himself more wrongs and righted nothing. He was appalled to remember he had called her name in public, in a desperate tone of voice – it could be the talk of Five Oaks. He must calm down, he had to go back to Emily and present her with the gifts he still carried, which had been downgraded from surprise into inadequate peace offerings.

He marched past Archer Street, he could not go home until he had mastered his nerves by means of strenuous physical activity. He was assuming he would not run into Carmen, but he did not know for sure where she was, and he was ready to deal with her should they meet. He would like to smack her, she deserved it, and he had no pity whatsoever for her 'death' in Rome. He was inclined to think she had played dead; but he could not explain her blue fingernails and her rapidly cooling body. Anyway, death seemed not to have done her much harm.

He walked for half an hour and felt able to face Emily. He entered the house, called her name, but received no answer. Unfairly, it annoyed him. He was not in a tolerant mood. Emily's note on the kitchen table, saying she would be late back, something to do with Anna, did not mollify.

It was about three o'clock. Emily arrived at seven. She told him Anna had a cough which could have been croup, and she and Susan had spent hours together at Dr Tomkins' surgery and then trying to find an out-of-hours pharmacy. He was not sympathetic, he could not concentrate on minor matters. Supper was a scratch meal prepared in a hurry, and the evening was more TV than talk.

In the bedroom he switched off his bedside light while she was in the bathroom. She entered quietly and switched off her light, too. He turned over twice, but sleep eluded him.

She spoke in a quiet voice.

'Are you cross with me, David?'

'No,' he replied.

'Are you all right?'

'I had a tiring day.'

'I'm sorry.'

'Not your fault. Are you quite well?'

'Yes and no.'

'What's wrong?'

'You seem to be so cross.'

'I'm not cross with you, not at all.'

'Are you cross with someone else?'

'No, I am not. Can we postpone this discussion? It's really beside the point.'

'What point?'

'Trying to get some sleep.'

'Good night, David.'

'Good night.'

The room was pitch-dark, and his temper was not improved by realising his answers had been oppressive.

'David?'

'Yes?'

'Is it because I didn't stay with you in Rome?'

'No, nothing to do with that – it's nothing to do with anything.'

'Will we ever make love again?'

'What?'

'I think you heard.'

'Of course we will.'

'When?'

'I don't know – when we feel like it – when you're ready – I don't mind.'

'What would you say if I said I was ready now?'

'Fine! That suits me.'

'Oh David...'

Perhaps she was protesting, she had been going

to procrastinate, but he was already climbing into her bed.

Their communing was brisk in spite of a temporary loss of his vigour. She gave him extra encouragement and he was savagely determined.

After they were back in their separate beds, she said: 'Thank you, David.'

He did not like the unusual formality, but mumbled that he should be thanking her.

'Good night, darling,' she said. 'Sleep well!'

'Same to you,' he said in a voice trying to be tender.

They did not speak again. He was relieved to have succeeded after fearing he would fail; on the other hand his unhappiness was deepened by his acknowledgment that what had been made was bad love, mechanical on his side, ineffectual on hers – she had not worked a miraculous cure. He lay sleepless in the dark room. Later on she might have sobbed, but the sob was either stifled or a cough.

CHAPTER SEVEN

November brought darkening days. The air grew colder, and wind-borne rain thumped against the windowpanes. Leaves blocked drains. The shortest day of the year was still a long way off, and spring was over the horizon. The charities rattled their boxes at every street corner.

David Crisp was racked with nostalgia. He remembered the excitement of his childhood at this time of year. He had been allowed to tear the page headed November, dreary November, from the calendar in the kitchen at Eastern Street, where the Crisps had lived before Saturn Street. But his memories of December were of Manor Crescent, of the festivities and fun Emily had made for himself, Gwen, Archie, sometimes Jane, and for Granpa Billy and Granma Marigold, and his own parents. She had worked night and day to decorate the Christmas tree, buy and pack presents for everyone, cook tremendous meals and spread cheer. He saw her laughing in a paper hat with stars, flushed, eyes shining, so proud of her family, so loving, so loved.

It was not only nostalgia he was racked by.

The David sitting by himself in the square of the Pantheon in Rome, in the sunlight before a shadow fell upon him, had known who he was, where he was and how he had got there, and where he expected to go. He was not a fool, he had no reason to doubt any of these assumptions. He was fit, clever enough, popular, part-owner of a business historically proof against the sling and arrows of politics, had a gem of a wife, and a daughter, son and grandchild. He was not greedy, nor was he oblivious to the main chance, he would expand Macer and Crisp if he could, he had his ambitions, but he knew his place in the world and was content to stand on his rung of the social ladder. He was proud to be a middling sort of man. The fact was that in his later forties he had possessed all that his heart could desire.

Inwardly, and repeatedly, he reeled off the above, which led to the rhetorical question: 'What had become of the man he had thought he was?'

The answer was crushingly negative. He had been stripped naked of more than clothes in the *Albergo Diurno*. Two points had been proved there, that he was strong in the virile sense, and feeble otherwise. He had broken rule after rule. What he had become was amoral, unrighteous, a leaf in the storm, a featherweight.

And his one act of love since then had been bitter as never before, hurtful rather than healing, and not even reliable. Oh yes, he was sorry; but he had too much to be sorry for, he did not know how to begin not having to be sorry for everything.

He teased himself with hackneyed phrases,

110

making a clean breast, for instance, grasping the nettle, facing the music, standing up and being counted.

He had thought about it, he had done his best not to think about it. He would be plunging a dagger into Emily's loving heart, dragging her innocence through mud, offending her perhaps irreparably, revealing that he was unworthy. She might even want to divorce him. He would have disgraced himself in the eyes of his parents, his children, his sister-in-law Jane – Jane would no longer be the sole black sheep in the family flock. His position in the society of Five Oaks would be forfeited, and there might be commercial consequences. He could be ruined by the diabolical divorce laws. He would have to consider his position, as they say – that is, decide whether to live or die.

His mental processes were nothing like thoughts containing a measure of sense and significance, they were like a mouse running in a wheel in a cage. The critical points for his physical constitution were the afternoon of the French Market, and especially his losing so much control that he ran after Carmen and shouted her name for all to see and hear; and the sequel with Emily. He caught a cold that turned into a peculiar sort of infection. He began to ache all over and his joints stiffened. He had never been ill before, he was humiliated by only being able to open a door with difficulty, dosed himself with aspirin in one form and aspirin in other forms, and agreed with Emily that he had better

111

have a word with Dr Tomkins. The compensation was that at last he had a real excuse for his behaviour.

The Crisps had been Dr Tomkins' patients for years. He had helped with the births of Gwen and Archie. He was an old friend and a reluctant civil servant in the medical department of the Whitehall bureaucracy. He called the Crisps by their Christian names while they all addressed him formally – it was a kind of joke between them.

He scolded David for not being as well as usual, and after a chat and a brief examination said that he suspected polymyalgia.

'What's that?' David asked.

'Instant rheumatics all over – I'll test your blood – not too serious and can be treated with steroids. It's contracted by elderly people after a shock to the system as a rule. Why have you at your age got it?'

'I don't know,' David replied, laughing in order to look less shifty.

'Haven't you been on holiday?'

'Yes – Rome – our silver wedding.'

'You're not looking as if you've been on holiday.'

'Sorry about that.'

They laughed.

'Oh yes,' Dr Tomkins said, 'Emily's father – he died, didn't he?'

'Yes.'

'Were you fond of him?'

'Very.'

'Would that account for it?'

'You're the doctor, Dr Tomkins.'

'I'll have the result of your test later today, and if it signals polymyalgia I'll have a prescription for steroids waiting for you at the surgery. I'm pretty sure I'm right.'

'Lucky you.'

'Every doctor spends most of his life worrying that he's wrong.'

Dr Tomkins was right, and Emily was pleased. She said to David: 'It explains a lot. I knew something was amiss. You'll soon be well, thank goodness! Dr Tomkins told me the pills are miraculous.'

David played the invalid after the pills had worked the minor miracle.

Life carried on at Manor Crescent, in Five Oaks, in the country and the world: how confusing it was for him that his personal cataclysm had had so little effect on the planet. His lies had not been seen through, he had not been unmasked, and, despite his guilt and Carmen, he had as good as got away with murder.

Gwen's weekend visits were brighter spots in the half-light of his existence. She came down from London for the weekend after he had begun to take his steroid pills, and they went for a walk in Richmond Park on Saturday afternoon while Emily was taking care of Anna. It was sunny and breezy weather, not cold, almost pleasant.

She said to him as they strolled along, sometimes with her arm linked in his: 'I don't feel I'm visiting the sick.'

'I'm fine,' he replied, and untypically he was annoyed to have used a cliché – Gwen deserved better than a fib – it was annoying not to be honest.

'Was there a cause I don't know about?'

'What do you mean?'

'Is there a hidden agenda, Dad?'

'Nothing like that.'

'Nothing to tell me?'

'I've always told you the truth, and I will, I will, when I can.'

'Is it bad?'

'No.'

'Important?'

'No.'

'Does Mum know?'

'No – it's nothing. Can we talk about you?'

'Well, I always like to do that – no secret there!'

They laughed.

'Is Hugh Traviss still bothering you?'

'No – as you would say.'

'A bit?'

'I can cope with Hugh.'

'Is there another man?'

'Of course.' They laughed again, and she added: 'Actually, two.'

'Two. You haven't wasted time.'

'They're only twinkles in my eye.'

'Peruvian twinkles?'

'Yes and no. You know I finished with Hugh ages before we separated. I was never unfaithful to him – he was professionally unfaithful. I knew one of my men in Peru.'

114

'And the other?'

'Well, he's half-Peruvian, but I met him in London – his father's English and I met him ten days ago.'

'What's the object of the exercise?'

'I'm lonely sometimes, I don't like being a spinster, and I'm warm-hearted. You know what I mean, Dad. I don't think I'm asking for the moon. I'd just like to be a wife and the mother of a few children.'

'You'll need a husband.'

'Exactly.'

'What sort are you looking for?'

They laughed again.

'One like you.'

'Oh no!'

'A kind one, a good one, like you, Dad – nothing incestuous.'

'I shouldn't be in the frame. You mustn't go by me. What are your young men called?'

'Sorry if I said something wrong, Dad.'

'It's all right. Tell me about them!'

'My Peruvian's Luis, spelt differently from English Lewis, and my half-Englishman's James. Luis is in high finance, James is a diplomat.'

'What are their characters?'

'Luis is exciting, James a bit stodgy. They're both nice, but Luis takes risks, and James might be boring although he's cleverer than me.'

'Is there a compromise candidate?'

'Not at the moment.'

'You'd have to settle in Peru if you chose Luis, and you'd be living all over the world if you were in the diplomatic service. We wouldn't see much of each other, and Emily would be sad not to help with your children.'

'That's part of the problem.'

'Are you at all committed?'

'No. It's what I long to be. But I haven't lifted a finger to beckon anyone. All that's happened so far is my thinking that if I made a move everything could happen. I really need guidance. I'm in the position of women who get desperate and rush in.'

'Don't, please! Be patient! You're such a lovely person, you're a tonic. Don't waste yourself!'

'Thank you, Dad.'

'I can't give guidance. I would if I could, but... Your mother made courtship so easy for me... I don't know much about love in a worldly modern way. I only know a mistake can have awful consequences.'

'How do you know about mistakes?'

'What?'

'How do you know about the awfulness?'

'Well – I've seen it, observed it, over and over again.'

'I suppose I have, too.'

They walked for a short distance in silence, then Gwen pointed to a herd of the Richmond Park red deer.

'I wouldn't mind being one of them,' she said. 'A hind's a lucky girl. She just settles for her strongest suitor in the rutting season, joins his harem, submits to his occasional and very brief attentions, bears or does not bear a baby, and has no emotional problems for most of the rest of every year, barring accidents.'

David said: 'Why not hang on for your strongest suitor?'

'Not a bad idea, Dad.'

On the way home Gwen asked again: 'Are you really on the mend?'

'Yes – I'm holding positive thoughts – yes, thanks.'

'Can we talk again?'

'Of course we can.'

'You can always talk to me.'

'You're such a dear girl.'

But she made him sadder. She reminded him of the sort of talks he was no longer having with Emily. And their wordless communicating was a thing of the past: now he had to cudgel his brains for a topic of conversation with his wife. The discussion of plans, which had been at least necessary and potentially interesting, struck him as burdensome and ominous: where were they going, might Carmen be there too? Sometimes, when he did have something to say, he suspected her of not listening to him, and then she would rebuke him for not listening to her.

Rheumatism had saved him from the snares of Venus, but convalescence did not encourage entanglement. One travesty of love had put both of them off. They rubbed along nonetheless. Emily seemed not to be unduly perturbed by the state of their relationship, and he concealed the fact that his heart was not in the life they were leading. His tension tired him. He was waiting for something to happen. He could not rid himself of the suspicions that he was sitting on a time bomb, and all his dear ones were at risk.

His son Archie arriving in his office in business hours was not the happening he expected. David set aside his work and conducted Archie into his sanctum.

'What brings you here?' he asked apprehensively.

Archie, sitting in the chair on the other side of the desk and looking too big for it, said in his usual genial manner: 'Not a crisis, Dad, nothing to worry about.'

David was relieved.

'Well, that's something,' he remarked.

Archie shifted on the chair.

'Sorry to bother you, Dad. It's a small matter, but you might think it's a big one. I hope you'll pardon me for not beating about the bush. Have you made a will?'

'That's an interesting question. I suppose it's grist to your mill?'

'Of course we do wills, solicitors do, but it's not that, I'm not trawling for your business. Granpa Hector gave me food for thought.'

'Oh yes?'

'You haven't answered my question, Dad.'

'No – true enough – here's my answer. I don't need to make a will. My sole heir is my next of kin, all I have will go to your mother.'

'Including the agency?'

'She'll have to take advice about the agency. She'll probably ask you for advice.'

'And I'd have homework – I know nothing about Macer and Crisp – it must be pretty valuable. And Mum could be caught for CGT or IHT, inheritance tax, payable on inherited money beyond a certain figure.'

'I know that, Archie – aren't you teaching your grandmother?'

'Sorry, Dad. I don't mean to be cheeky – honestly! I was only wondering...'

'Wondering what?'

'If you might consider the possibility of making a will and at the same time handing over a sum of money to the next generation in order to minimise the tax.'

'Anna, for example?'

'Maybe other children, too.'

'Other children of yours?'

'Well, yes.'

'Is Susan pregnant?'

'We're not sure, she could be.'

'You're a fertile couple.'

'Thanks, Dad.'

'What about Gwen?'

'She's not married.'

'Not yet, but her children if or when she has any would have the same rights as Anna and her brothers and sisters.'

'I'm not trying to do Gwen out of anything.'

'No – I'm sure you're not – you're too nice to do such a thing.'

'I tell clients every day what I'm telling you, Dad. It's sensible. Gifts are tax-free after a number of years.'

'Listen, I'm confident your mother will distribute our money as she thinks fit and fairly.'

'Nobody can see into the future. And nothing in writing spells trouble.'

'I'm sorry, Archie. Has it occurred to you that you might be jumping the gun? Why the urgency?'

'It's not urgent, Dad – Susan and I hope and believe you'll live to be as old as Granpa – it's just that we have noticed how tired you've been looking, and you had that nasty turn in the taxi and now the polymyalgia.'

'You shouldn't tell people they look tired.'

'Oh – sorry!'

'I've still got one foot out of the grave.'

'Oh Dad! There was something else. I hear you chased after a woman when the French Market was in the High Street.'

'How did you hear that?'

'Leslie Robins told me, he's my colleague. He said you were pretty upset.'

'I don't want you gossiping about it to your mother, Archie. You make it sound worse than it was. I can explain it for your ears, but I don't like having to justify myself.'

'No offence meant.'

'Or taken. I wasn't "chasing" a woman. I was trying to hand over a document to a female client – she'd left it in the office.'

'Did you catch her?'

'No – but it didn't matter – she's quite scatty.'

'Who is she?'

'Who? She's Joe Macer's client. I think she's called Carner or Car-something. Anyway, Archie,

I'll ponder your suggestions. Thanks for your trouble. Now we've both got business to see to.'

'Understood! I was only asking, Dad.'

David, alone in his sanctum, mopped his brow. He felt shaken – Archie had shaken the kaleidoscope. While the father was struggling to prop up and reconstitute his life, the son was advising him to prepare for death. Surely he was not in such bad shape? That was the question. But he had no time to answer, clients with appointments were waiting in the shop to talk to him.

He was still trying to answer all the questions and to absorb the shocks of his interview with Archie when, some days or, rather, some nights later, he had a nightmare. He dreamt of Carmen. And dreams, like sex in action, have no conscience. He woke to new regrets that he had again responded to her charms. The frontier was not crossed, but he feared that it would have been if he had not woken. The fact was that he had had an adulterous experience within an arm's length of his wife. He felt at least emotionally soiled. He felt he was a double traitor. His overriding thought was that for both their sakes, Emily's and his own, he could not go on in this way for much longer.

More days passed. He arrived in the office one morning and was approached by Joe Macer. Joe was younger than David. In his early forties, he was the image of a reliable estate agent, fresh complexioned to show he led a virtuous life, seriously bespectacled, soft-voiced and with a ready smile. He was wanting decisions from David. The architect's plan for the modernisation of the premises was running out of time – they could soon be charged a cancellation fee. And were they or were they not to advertise for the extra secretary?

David said: 'I'm sorry, I've been remiss – one thing after another – you know how it is.'

'I know you lost your father-in-law, but that was some time ago.'

'Was it? Yes, I suppose it was.'

'Pardon me for asking, are you in any sort of trouble?'

'No, certainly not. What makes you think so?'

'Well – your attention to business has wandered a bit lately. We hear a lot about mid-life crises nowadays, don't we?'

'I'll sharpen up.'

'And I'm ready to lend a hand if need be.'

In the afternoon of that same day David rang Max Harrison.

Max's greeting was racy, jolly, out of date, and descriptive of himself: 'How's tricks?'

'I'm sliding downhill,' David replied.

'What's become of the fighting spirit of the Crisps?'

'I wasn't ever a fighter, Max. I was born a pacifist, I just had luck, good turns fell into my lap.'

'I've had a gaggle of women crying on my shoulder, I always doled out sympathy in bed. Can't do the same for you, old boy. What's the score?'

'No more luck.'

'Are you having a nervous breakdown?'

'You're the second person to ask me today. The other person called it a mid-life crisis.'

'What was your reply?'

'It was "no, not I". Now it's "probably".'

'Who's doing you down?'

'The usual one, myself. I can't tell you. The facts that matter are that I committed a kind of crime with an accomplice, and the accomplice is now hunting me and has the power to destroy my family.'

'A member of the weaker sex, of course?'

'Weaker or stronger.'

'What does she want?'

'I don't know.'

'Money?'

'I don't think so.'

'What then?'

'Reunion, sex maybe.'

'Can't you see her off?'

'Not at the moment – she's the skeleton in my cupboard. My secret is her power.'

'You were a good boy too long, David. If everybody thinks you're bad, like me, you can't get into more trouble than you're already in. Sex isn't a crime, it may be a misdemeanour or a mistake. It doesn't amount to much if you think about it in cold blood. Women know that, so do gynaecologists, but women ring-fence it with mystiques to keep Tom, Dick and Harry at bay.'

'I couldn't tell Emily that sort of stuff.'

'What did you mean when you said you couldn't see this woman off at the moment?'

'I haven't confessed yet.'

'Is that your big idea?'

'I can't see my way round it.'

'Honesty isn't always the best policy.'

'What's the alternative?'

'Tact.'

'You're muddling me, Max.'

'That gloomy old Norwegian – what's his name? – Ibsen, wrote plays about people who always told the truth and ruined lots of lives. Truth versus tact – it's a close-run thing. Tact without lying might come out on top.'

'All I know for sure is that I'm near the end of my tether.'

'Chin up, old boy! It'll all be the same in a hundred years.'

'No more proverbs, Max!'

'Well – I have spoken. I'd better add that my marriages are not proof of my knowing how to handle a woman. You'll pull through, I bet.'

David was unconvinced. He lived in limbo, pretending he was not waiting for the flash of lightning and the crash of thunderstorm. His nerves jangled privately, and he imagined his blood pressure was dangerously high.

The crisis would have been funny if he had retained any of his old sense of humour. It happened in his lunch hour on a working weekday. His habit was either to pop in for a scratch meal at The Five Barrels, round the corner from Macer and Crisp, or else to have sandwiches sent in

124

from the pub to the office. On the day in question he had time for a meal, he would be on his own, Joe and colleagues had plans of their own, and he collected some business letters and papers, bagged a table in a dark corner of the restaurant area, ordered steak and kidney pie, bought half a pint of bitter, and began to read. There were places for twenty-five or so in this part of the pub, and people were already seated there and more customers came in. They chattered, musak played, chairs and bar-stools scraped on the boarded floor, and David concentrated on his reading matter. He drank some beer, his plate of pie arrived and he began to eat it, and because it was difficult to read and eat at the same time he looked up and round at the people at other tables.

Carmen was there. She was three tables away from where he sat. Her back was turned, but she was unmissable. Black curls tumbled round her shoulders, she seemed to be wearing the same tight-fitting jacket that had revealed her neat little waist at the French Market. She was with a man, he was nothing like the one who had escorted her into the Dorchester Hotel, so far as David could see he was a country type, tieless and wearing a brown corduroy jacket. They were talking together with some animation – David remembered that when he was with her it had been less talk and more do.

Old and new questions were swept aside while his obsessive train of thought ousted other reactions. What she was doing in The Five Barrels was to tease and challenge him again. She must have tracked him to the pub, and was intending to show him her face and frighten him. The anger of a tolerant man, the desperate anger of a trapped creature, the careless rage of utter exasperation, took hold of him, and without further consideration, on impulse, he stood up, strode across to where she sat, flourishing papers in his left hand, and laid his free right hand on her shoulder and squeezed.

She cried out and twisted round – not Carmen – a ruddy-faced farm girl – and her companion was lumbering to his feet.

David was sorry – how sorry he was! – he had thought she was someone else – he was almost in tears – he hurried towards the exit, calling to the landlord to offer drinks at his expense to the couple he pointed at.

He walked away from the pub, his office, his home, Five Oaks, anybody who might recognise him, down to the River Thames that moved majestically and without hesitation towards the sea. He still clutched his papers, he had lost everything except his papers, his way, and his wits. He could kill Carmen, she was to blame for all that was wrong with him and his life. How extraordinarily awful that she had brought him so low, him of all people, as to assault a stranger in a public place! He had squeezed that girl's shoulder with all the strength of his fingers – his fingers had dug into her – he must have hurt her – but he was sure he was more hurt than she was.

He returned to Macer and Crisp at about four o'clock. He entered the shop, limped in metaphorically, like a shamefaced dog that had stayed out too late. Joe Macer was with a client, but glanced at David with a shadowy frown: more lies needed to be told. He found a list of telephone calls he was meant to return, and a dozen faxes requiring answers, and he looked at his watch. The shop would close in an hour. He could deal with most of the business matters in the morning, he was definitely not up to talking mortgages, completion dates, gazumping and changed minds at the present time. He scribbled the text of faxes that Alice could type and send.

At five o'clock he emerged from his sanctum, mumbled an excuse in passing to Joe – 'I couldn't get away from a client this afternoon' – and headed home. The unease that afflicted him in the company of his wife had been superseded by his crying need to be in familiar surroundings and even with Emily, in her pure atmosphere, within the glow of her benevolence. She was out. She had left a message on the doormat to say she had gone to help at the hospital with the casualties of a rail crash.

He cursed inwardly. He was not in an altruistic mood. He hoped the injuries of the victims of the crash were not going to detain her and leave him high and dry – and hungry – he had eaten nothing except a mouthful of pie since breakfast. But six o'clock arrived slowly, and seven seemed to drag its feet. He thought of ringing Gwen or Max; but overwrought fathers should not call for mercy from their daughters, and he required solace from the opposite of a womaniser. He tried in vain to pray, he lost track of set prayers, and he felt he had no right to ask God to help to clean up his mess.

Emily returned at a quarter past eight. She had seen such haunting sights, she had been consoling so many very sad people, she was sorry to be late, but she would fix up some supper as soon as possible.

'Don't hurry,' he said.

'I couldn't leave before – they were short-handed – and stretcher-bearers queued to get into the hospital – it was heart-breaking, David.'

'There's no rush. And you must be exhausted.'

'Would you mind if I changed my clothes? I think I'm covered with blood.'

'Of course.'

He waited more patiently. He not only admired her for what she had been doing – she was not a nurse, her work at the hospital was voluntary and menial – he was also touched by her consideration of himself after all she had been through.

She reappeared and cooked him a fillet of plaice and made a salad. She was not hungry, she ate salad and a tiny bit of cheese. He finished his meal with an apple, and they adjourned to the sitting-room.

They sat on their usual chairs, as they habitually did to watch the news on TV. But he did not switch on the TV, and she began to sob and cry. She had been near tears at the kitchen table, and had had no more to say to him than he had to say to her. Now he embraced her and offered comforting words. The scene was prologued, she kept on referring to the injuries. His thoughts took off at a tangent. He remembered the love that had been made in their home. He remembered sex that was an extension of their love, their choice of each other, life together, parenthood, friendship and mutual support. Lust was something else. Carmen was a shadow compared with the real woman in his arms, whose anatomy he knew by heart.

She said she was going to call it a day. They stood and he embraced her.

'I love you,' he said.

She looked up at him with the tears in her eyes, and smiled and thanked him. The wonderful thing was that she did not refer to their estrangement, she was neither probing nor ironic, she accepted his declaration at its face value.

He hugged her, she hugged him, and again she looked up at him with a smile and said: 'But I think I'll go to sleep as soon as my head touches the pillow.'

He got the message.

'Yes, yes,' he said. 'Go to bed, darling. I'll creep in later without waking you.'

CHAPTER EIGHT

At moments David Crisp so far forgot himself as to think he was in the clear and nothing too bad had happened and nothing worse was on the cards. Sometimes he awoke from dreams of innocence. But mostly he felt as if danger in the form of a big cat was stalking him and preparing to pounce. He had already been mauled more than once.

Jane returned to 12 Manor Crescent. Was his sister-in-law a big cat? Metaphorically he recoiled when he opened the front door and saw her grinning at him and expecting to be admitted. She had done her disappearing act after her father's funeral and since then had not made a sign of life. Of course she had left belongings in the spare room, she had only taken with her what Emily called an 'action pack'. Where she had gone, and who she had gone with or to, was not known. Both Crisps were sure she would be back, but under pressure of events had more or less forgotten to remember. David accepted her greeting of a shriek and a rather wet kiss while he mentally estimated the costs of another invasion, and Emily dropped a saucepanful of boiled potatoes when her sister entered the kitchen.

At least Jane announced on the Friday evening that she would not be staying long, even if she said it ungraciously.

'Great news, I'll be relieving you of my company on Monday morning, yes, this Monday coming – you'll only have to suffer me for three days and nights.'

They laughed it off. They laughed her off when she laughed at them for being stick-in-the-muds, churchgoers, and small town smugginses. But in fact she was not much trouble for most of the time. She was meeting old friends who were still friendly for lunch on the Saturday and Sunday, and she was invited to supper with the Archies on the Saturday. David was glad not to see much of her; and only knew via Emily that she had made a new friend, lover, protector, sugar-daddy, or simply lonely old widower, who had invited her to accompany him on a cruise round the world. She was therefore more excited than difficult. She was also busy, fitting in hair-dos, beauty treatments, last minute shopping – their liner sailed from Southampton on the Tuesday.

The Crisps were having dinner with Jane on the Sunday, her last night in Five Oaks and in England for the foreseeable future. It was a sort of celebration for one reason or another. They drank wine before the meal, then Emily went into the kitchen to put finishing touches to her cooking.

As soon as her back was turned, Jane said to David: 'Well, now, brother-in-law, what have you been up to?'

His heart sank. He tried to make a joke of it.

He said: 'What are you up to, that's what I'd like to know?'

'Who's Carmen?'

'Sorry?'

'Who's the bit of skirt you ran after in the High Street?'

'She is not what you're suggesting, and I wasn't doing what you're suggesting. She is a Macer and Crisp client, she'd left an important piece of paper in the office, and I was hoping to give it back to her. She does not have the name you mention.'

'What is her name?'

'She's not my client, I scarcely know her, she's Mrs Carden or Carbourne.'

'Not what I've been told.'

'You shouldn't come and stay in our house, Jane, and dredge gossip out of the gutters that's inaccurate and libellous.'

'Ho-hum, David! I hope for my sister's sake you're not sneaking into the big league.'

'What's that?'

'That's where the fun is, it is where good little people are usually not admitted.'

'But you have a season ticket?'

'Sure thing!'

'Don't make mischief, Jane! If you do you'll never see the inside of this house again.'

Emily called them into the kitchen. Supper did not go with much of a swing. Jane had things to attend to upstairs and an early start tomorrow morning. They said their good nights and goodbyes. When David kissed Jane and she had embraced him in her typical way, too close, she bent back, looked up and into his face and winked one of her eyes. He repulsed her. He objected to the wink and hoped Emily had not seen it – he hoped she too would not ask him for explanations.

He was lucky for a change. There were no matrimonial repercussions after Jane's departure. But David was more wretched inside. He felt he was almost in reach of the big cat. The Wednesday of that week arrived, half-day for the shops of Five Oaks, and he was unwilling to go home, unable to go to the pub where he might find or be found by the girl whose shoulder he had squeezed and her vengeful boyfriend, and altogether hemmed in and persecuted. He sent out for a sandwich, then rang his parents, and in due course arrived in Saturn Street. His mother welcomed him and gave him tea in the kitchen. His father joined them, and they talked of old times quietly and, so far as David was concerned, soothingly. His parents said they were well, and how was he?

David hesitated, then frustrated his sudden desire to tell the whole truth by mentioning Jane. He answered their questions, and heard himself exaggerating the inconvenience of Jane in order to account for his sombre mood.

'I counted the blessing of having been an only child,' he said.

'Well, I'm glad of that,' his mother commented;

'all the same, I would have liked to have another child, a daughter.'

'Did something go wrong?'

'Ask your father!'

'What's the meaning of that, Dad?'

'Nothing to speak of.'

'It wasn't nothing to speak of at the time,' Gloria said.

'It was a long time past – water under the bridge.'

'Oh well, that's true.'

David intervened.

'Half a mo! This is news to me. What are you telling me?'

'It doesn't matter, dear.'

'I'm very interested.'

His parents looked at each other calmly, Gloria so small considering how big David was, sitting upright on the edge of her chair, and Hector with his white thatch of hair and carpenter's hands folded across his cardigan and smiling without embarrassment.

Hector confessed: 'I misbehaved myself.'

Gloria explained: 'He went with another woman after you were born, and I wouldn't let him near when we might have been breeding.'

'You amaze me.'

They all laughed.

'Everybody makes mistakes, don't they, David?' Hector said.

'They do.'

'I forgave him in the end,' Gloria said.

'Was it difficult?'

135

'I always loved him, you see, and he said he loved me. Women are born to take the rough with the smooth.'

Hector said: 'I had it rough for a bit, if it comes to that – taught me a lesson, I suppose.'

David spoke again.

'I've always thought of you two as the ideal couple, never looking to right or left. You made us happy by being so happy yourselves.'

Hector said: 'That's your mother's doing.'

And Gloria contradicted and confirmed.

'I don't take the credit, I couldn't, it was providence that I won your father in the lottery – I mean, lottery of life – and we've been comfortable for fifty years. The difficulty we had, it proved how nice it was to be easy with each other.'

The subject changed, they had to chat about Christmas – his parents intended to feed neighbours with turkey and plum pudding but accepted an invitation to tea at Five Oaks on Boxing Day. David chatted while his head whirled. His parents' experience of adultery had a bearing on his own. Could his present misery ever become a footnote to the story of another golden wedding? Hope flickered in the inner darkness. But a draught of realities blew it out. Carmen was not 'a woman', Emily might not be so philosophic as his mother, and his temperament was less philosophical than his father's. Three wrongs could not make a right in his estimation.

He said he had to be going. He was abrupt, his mother noticed, and she held his hand as they walked along the passage to the front door.

'Thank you for paying us compliments, dear boy. Is Emily well, not counting Jane?'

'I think so.'

'Give her my love, our love, won't you?'

'Yes, Ma.'

'Providence has been good to you, too.'

'I know.'

'Does Emily know?'

'What?'

'Does she know providence has been good to her?'

He laughed and replied: 'I wouldn't like to say so. She's a lovely person.'

'She is – and valuable. Give her a kiss as well from me.'

'Thanks, Ma.'

'Don't feel obliged to come and see us. We're okay.'

'But I love to see you.'

'Yes, same here.'

He and his father shook hands, and he drove back to Manor Crescent without hurrying.

A few days later David had another talk that circled round the matter uppermost in his mind. It was accidental. Emily had cut ivy off their garden wall and he offered to run it round to St Anne's, where some parishioners were decorating the church for the Christmas services. Sam Wilcomb was alone there, waiting for a second team of decorators to arrive. David delivered the ivy, Sam thanked him and sat down on a nearby pew, saying his feet were punishing him for his sins. He explained that he was not spared a 'Christmas rush' of a religious nature.

David said: 'I'm sure your sins aren't unforgivable.'

Sam replied: 'I hope not – but you never know – sin is redefined through the ages – modern sins are so sinful that the ancients never dreamt of them, let alone condemned them.'

'What are the "deadly" sins, Sam?'

'The monks worked them out in the dark ages. There are seven – pride, covetousness, lust, envy, gluttony, anger, sloth. Murder's not included, nor is mass-murder, which is different and worse, nor is genocide. Murder was forbidden later on, but lust got off more lightly – sins of the flesh were wrong but natural. The theory of "original sin", that Adam and Eve were created with their very own streak of wickedness, which all of us inherit, was a great help in explaining our inclination to err and stray. Of course the liberals are against it, they oppose it completely, they want nothing whatsoever to be the fault of anybody, they think we all ought to win the prizes.'

'I wish you'd preach a sermon about sin.'

'Is Five Oaks ready for my description of hell-fire, where some of us and our neighbours may soon be sizzling?'

They laughed.

David said: 'I wish we still had Confession and Absolution in our church – I think they must have been useful.'

'The Roman Catholic Church only does Confession if it's specially requested nowadays.'

'Really?'

'Why are you interested in sin, David?'

'Oh – I don't know – I'm not a pious person – I'm not so religious as Emily, and never have been – but what else is there?'

'That's a question and a half.'

'It's not important, Sam – forget it!'

'Does something weigh on your mind?'

'Yes – life! – no, nothing in particular.'

'You could come and talk to me.'

'Thanks, Sam. I'd just waste your time. I've been wasting it – and here come your ladies to twirl the ivy round your pulpit.'

The accumulated weight on David's mind was that he had lied to Sam Wilcomb and before that to his mother, wife, son, daughter, sister-in-law, doctor and colleagues. He felt himself sinking deeper and deeper into a quicksand of untruthfulness. Other marine metaphors applied to him: out of his depth, lost his bearings, all at sea, on the rocks. That the sins of the flesh had not been considered deadly, and that he might have followed in his father's errant footsteps, were items of subsidiary interest.

Were his honesty, dependability, gone for good?

The point was, and the truth maybe, that he could not depend on himself. He yearned to be worthy of Emily, to deserve to be offered a second chance to live with her in peace and harmony, yet was not certain he could refuse and repudiate Carmen.

139

His apprehensiveness had not decreased – because of the alarmingly grey area in his psychology between how he should and how he would behave if confronted by the latter, it gained ground with every passing day.

Contrariness was not the least of his anxieties. He clung to his marriage, theoretically it was his panacea, but the chores of home were causing him more pain than pleasure. He had no time for gardening, and no patience for housework. He wished to conserve his energy for his lonely struggle with demons, not to waste it on banal events and petty crises.

Gwen's telephone call was full of sweet concern and exciting news, but also aggravating. She rang him one afternoon at the office.

'Dad, I'm breaking unwritten laws,' she said.

'Hullo, darling,' he returned.

'I shouldn't be ringing you at work.'

'It doesn't matter. How are you?'

'Have you got a little time, Dad?'

'I have – it's late enough, I'll be shutting up shop soon – but I've always time for you. You haven't told me how you are.'

'Very well – I'll come to that in a minute – first of all, how are you? Seriously, Dad, I've been wondering.'

'I'm all right.'

'You always say that. You and I keep our trouble to ourselves. I probably worried you by telling you not to worry about me in Peru. Are you in any sort of trouble, Dad? I'd love to help if I could.'

He laughed and said: 'Thank you, darling Gwen. It's a wonderful offer, but you can't help me.'

'Is something wrong?'

'Yes and no. It'll blow over.'

'Does Mum...?'

'No.'

'Does she wish she did know?'

'I can't answer for her.'

'Is it very personal, Dad?'

'You could say so.'

'Not illness?'

'No.'

'Is it going to be a secret for ever?'

'Curiosity killed the cat.'

'You could just answer that question – is it like the secret of the Sphinx?'

'Yes.'

'We'll never know?'

'I hope not.'

'I'm so sorry you're in trouble, and I can't share it.'

'You're running ahead of me. I haven't said I'm in trouble. Can we change the subject, darling?'

'Sorry to be nosy, too.'

'I don't mind your nosiness.'

'You won't forget my offer, will you?'

'No, Gwen. Now, how well is very well?'

'Extremely!'

'I'm the curious one.'

'Could I bring someone to tea?'

'Yes – provisionally – I'll have to check dates with Mummy. Is it a friend of yours?'

'It is.'

'Is it male or female?'

'Male. It's a man, Dad.'

'Good heavens!'

'I'm not sure about heaven yet. I'm only bringing him to tea in case he embarrasses me and you don't take to him.'

'Is he the diplomat?'

'Yes.'

'That's a mercy! I dreaded a reckless son-in-law.'

'I dread a husband you didn't like. I don't think I could ever marry one. I want to make up for Hugh.'

'Hugh's neither here nor there, I hope.'

'I'm not rebounding, if that's what you mean. I rebounded from Hugh three years ago.'

'What's the diplomat's name?'

'James Chubb. My initials wouldn't change.'

'Not a good reason to marry.'

'I do love him.'

'Are you ready and willing to be a diplomatic gipsy?'

'The ready and willing bit's okay.'

'What about moving house every few years or even months, and mostly abroad?'

'I like abroad – but what about my children? They won't have chosen to be diplomatic.'

'Children don't choose. They learn to make the best of things. Can you manage James when he loses his temper?'

'He doesn't lose it.'

'Does he like dogs?'

'Yes – he says he could have one if he had a wife.'

'Any private means?'

'Enough – enough for two, he says.'

'Do you believe him?'

'Yes.'

'Where is he working now?'

'In London, in the Foreign Office.'

'That's something – you could start married life in this country – and we could see one another.'

'No, Dad – part of the problem is that he's being sent to Madrid.'

'Madrid after Peru, so soon after Peru?'

'It's a step up the ladder.'

'How long is the posting in Madrid?'

'A few years.'

'Oh dear!'

'I could easily fly home to see you, and you and Mum could stay with us.'

'Have you said yes?'

'We're on approval.'

'Are you happy, Gwen?'

'Potentially. If you approved, you and Mum, I would be.'

'Well, I'm potentially happy for you.'

They suggested a few dates for the tea party. She said: 'Jamie will love you both, as I do.'

'Ditto, my dear, as I love you, we both love you.'

He rang off and resolved not to be selfish. He had waited so long for Gwen to come home and give him back her sweetness, and now she was sailing over his horizon with James Chubb;

but it was her life. His heart ached not only for himself – Emily was going to be stricken, no Gwen available for more years, and none of Gwen's children to nurse and love, except in snatches. Madrid was not far over the horizon, but where next, Central Africa, Korea?

Joe Macer knocked on the door of his sanctum and asked: 'I'm locking up, or will you, David?'

David replied: 'I'm leaving, you lock up. Good night, Joe.'

'Night-night.'

It was nearly six o'clock, and dark out of doors. He needed time in which to brace himself for breaking the news at home. He also reflected that he had dropped too many hints to Gwen, had almost spilt the beans, and that he would have to solve his problem without further delay if he was to support Emily and make the most of Gwen, her wedding, and remaining days in England. Events in Five Oaks had overtaken events in Rome. He had chosen to walk the long way round to Manor Crescent, now he hurried – he was determined to be with Emily or to be waiting for her when she walked in.

He was in Union Road, about to turn into Archer Street, when the door of one of the cars parked there swung open as he approached, the interior light switched on, and a woman in the driving seat was looking up at him and saying, 'Hullo!'

She had her hair in curls, as before.

He was startled, and conscious of all sorts of nervous responses, but not shattered, not paralysed

144

– he had rehearsed the situation so often in his imagination.

'What do you want?' he asked.

'A few minutes.'

'Not here,' he said.

'I'll drive you somewhere.'

'Ten minutes at most,' he said.

'I promise.'

He sat in the car and the inside light switched off. She drove him to the free car park in North Road, where working people driving home had vacated spaces. She extinguished the car's headlights. They had talked while she drove.

'I thought you were dead.'

'I was only ill. When I came to, you'd gone.'

'Why are you hunting me? It's got to stop.'

'I won't kill you.'

'Thanks! I have a wife and children—'

She interrupted: 'I know. I won't hurt them. I want to apologise for dying.'

He did not laugh.

'Is that all?'

'Not quite. It was exciting in Rome, wasn't it? You enjoyed yourself.'

'No, Carmen—'

'You can't deny it. I have my memories. But we have unfinished business. Don't you remember the way I was lying?'

'No, Carmen—'

'Yes!' She interrupted again. 'If you'd accept my apology, and we could seal an agreement with a special sort of kiss, I'd leave you alone for ever after.'

'Nothing doing,' he said. 'Who are you anyway? I saw you one day with another man, going into the Dorchester Hotel, who was he? I could hunt you, too. I could contact that other man.'

'I'm Carmen to you.'

'That's all nonsense.' He reached for the door handle, but could not find it.

'Here,' she said.

He thought she was offering a means of opening the passenger door, he was confused as to what she was doing, but when he looked back at her she handed him a scrap of material, silky stuff, her knickers once more.

'Out of the question,' he said, throwing the item back at her.

She began to talk fast. Her eyes glittered in the lights of another vehicle passing by. She was telling him how they could fornicate there and then, in the dark, in the back seat, behind the smoked windows of her car. She was describing what he could do to her and she could do for him in language that was coarse as well as biological. He was talking at the same time and trying not to listen. He was saying: 'How do I open this door? Open it for me! No, no, shut up! That's disgusting. Let me out of here!' There was a brief physical exchange, her hands took liberties, and he pushed her away. At last she slumped in her seat, as if to say, 'Pax!'

What she did say was: 'It would have been so nice.'

'Not for me,' he replied. 'You rose from the dead, but you've been nearly the end of me.

Goodbye, Carmen! Adultery's all about death. I've learnt it the hard way, and I'm not dying for you.'

'Don't go!'

'Don't follow me! If you do, I'll get my wife to deal with you. How does this door open?'

She gave in, she opened her door, and the interior light switched on. He found the lever, stepped out, but held the door open, took the display handkerchief out of his top pocket, and wiped the inner door handle, then the outer one. She watched him, and at last he looked at her. She was very pretty, not young but ageless, and had a beautiful mouth, well-formed lips, a half-smile and white teeth. He would not weaken.

He said: 'Go away! There are no fingerprints on your car. Go – I'll watch you – and if you don't drive away I'll summon the police.'

'You're very English,' she said.

He slammed the door and walked into the shadows of Archer Street. Her car's headlights flashed on, and she drove past and out of sight.

He hurried on to Manor Crescent – he did not want to be late. He told Emily – told her that Gwen was probably going to marry a diplomat and, tactfully but in realistic terms, that they were gaining a son-in-law but losing a daughter. Her responses were three-fold. Her eyes betrayed momentary sadness, she was then impatient to ring Gwen to confirm the date for tea and to provide motherly encouragement, and finally she embraced David in a comforting manner.

She was better than he was, he thought. Her

reactions were more generous than his own. He felt small. His self-esteem seemed to hit the bottom of the glass. He was proud of nothing, and his meeting with Carmen was somehow a red herring, although it had caused his nerves to jangle and his whole physique to tremble.

Emily spoke to Gwen for a long time. He cooked sausages and mash for supper. They looked at the news on TV, and went to bed in turn. He kissed her good night and she switched off her bedside light. They had not discussed any of the outstanding matters between them, and love had not had its say.

Emotion welled up in David. All the repression in him was swept aside. He could not control his breathing, and was surprised that it did not wake Emily or cause comment. In an undertone he spoke her name.

She did not answer at once. He was deeply disappointed. He did not know whether or not to try again. Her answer, 'Yes?' was spoken in a quiet clear voice.

'I have something...'

She waited and then repeated, 'Yes?'

'Something to say about Rome...'

She waited and said: 'What is it, David?'

'I don't know how to say it.'

'Something happened in Rome, is that it?'

'Yes – no – you mustn't help me – it's my responsibility.'

'David, you're worrying me.'

'Sorry – yes! In Rome, on the day you left, I went into a place I shouldn't have gone into.'

148

'Was it a brothel?'

'No. A woman invited me.'

'A prostitute?'

'No – an English woman, I think she was playing a game.'

'What do you mean?'

'I don't know – it was all peculiar – she was acting like Carmen, the Spanish girl in a book.'

'Were you doing what I imagine you were?'

'Yes.'

There was a long pause.

'How can I ever trust you?'

'I don't know, I don't know.'

'I'd like to hit you. I'd like to kick you.'

'Shall I go on?' he asked.

'Yes.'

'She died.'

'What?'

'The woman suddenly died. I thought I'd be had up for murder.'

'David!'

'She wasn't dead – she was dead by all the signs and tests – not breathing so far as I could make out, no pulse, growing colder, nothing – but she'd had a stroke, I believe, a cataleptic stroke.'

'What's that?'

'A stroke that resembles death.'

'How do you know?'

'I got it from a medical dictionary.'

'Not nice for you.'

'No.'

'But you deserved it.'

149

'Yes. I thought of jumping into the Tiber, that evening in Rome.'

'Is that why I couldn't get you on the telephone?'

'Yes.'

Another pause.

She burst out: 'How can this be happening to me? Am I dreaming?'

'I wish you were.'

'How could you after ... after all we've been to each other?'

'I don't know, I can't tell you, I can't blame anyone else.'

'How did you find out she was alive?'

'Later – here in England – I was beginning to think I was okay – nobody had contacted me, no policeman, I mean – and I hadn't caught any disease. She was walking into the Dorchester Hotel.'

'In London?'

'In Park Lane.'

'What were you doing in Park Lane?'

'I'd been seeing Mum and Dad, and was in a taxi – I just happened to see her stepping out of a car.'

'Alone?'

'No, with a man – husband probably – looked like an ambassador – and she had none of her Carmen costume or the curly hair or the make-up.'

'What did you feel?'

'Awful – threatened – not sure I had seen straight. I was afraid she might look for me.'

'Was it when you fainted?'

'Yes.'

'And I sympathised!'

'You were lovely to me.'

'Don't talk about love!'

'Shall I go on?'

'You might as well.'

'I felt hunted.'

'Were you hunted?'

'It doesn't matter.'

'It does to me.'

'Yes.'

'When?'

'Twice. She traced me through the Hotel Universal. She was in Five Oaks on the afternoon of the French Market.'

'Did you meet her?'

'I saw her. I was angry – I tried to reach her and tell her off, but she escaped. She didn't know I'd seen her.'

'The other time?'

'This afternoon.'

'Oh no!'

'I talked to her for five minutes in her car – she'd been waiting for me, she accosted me. It was never anything important, and now it's zero. She'll never bother either of us again.'

'That's what you think!'

'I meant in person – knocking on our door, things like that.'

'How can you be sure?'

'I rejected her. She was playing a game and I wouldn't play, I opted out. I said I'd contact her husband.'

'Do you know his name, or hers?'

'She doesn't know that I don't know their names. I could possibly get them from the Dorchester. They're history, even if she isn't as dead as she was.'

'What is she to you, David?'

'A nightmare.'

'Is she pretty?'

'That wasn't the point.'

Silence fell. He was afraid she was crying.

He was desperately refusing to believe that he was being rejected. He summoned all depleted resources in order to plead with her.

'Can I finish?'

'No details – I don't want to hear.'

'About you, you're the essential part.'

'Me? Me! I thought ... I thought I was...'

'Emily, please, let me – everything I've said is the cause, not the effect. Listen! My unfaithfulness was everything bad, not to mention the biggest mistake of my life. It was on impulse, sin on a whim, but no less bad, no extenuating factor. The aftermath for me in Rome was paralysis. I couldn't think straight, I could only feel fear, fear of retribution, of being caught and punished, of past and future. In time that turned into the far greater fear of hurting and losing you. At least my mistake made me into the most faithful husband that ever was or could or would be.'

She was silent. He waited, striving to control distress and physical stress.

She whispered: 'I am listening.'

He said: 'I want us to be as we used to be,

as happy as we were, as I was – of course I want it – who wouldn't? But I feel bound to warn you that I'm not exactly the same. Sorry if that sounds threatening – no threat, Emily! The vows I made to you in church were serious, and I rue the day I broke them and always will. We were young then, and our marriage was romantic – you were all romance for me. The difference now is no doubt connected with Rome, with penitence, and a kind of punishment that fitted the crime, heartache and homesickness. Commitment is my new feeling for you and our family, but mainly for you. Gwen said the other day that she longed to commit herself to a man, and it struck me that I was committed. I promise I'm not putting pressure on you, and won't ever do so. I've told you what I want, but it's not what I expect. My apology is not meant to be egoism. They say it compounds a mistake by telling your wife you made it. My aim is to heal the wounds I've inflicted, if possible. What happens to us, God knows. I love you so much, Emily.'

He broke off, he had to, and waited in the dark room for her to pass sentence. He waited and waited.

She said: 'Oh David, David...'

She began to cry. He was speechless, he would have dissolved if he had tried to speak. He had lost the right to kiss her better. Again he waited, not breathing properly, all his muscles tensed.

She said in a voice full of tears: 'How can I forgive ... How can I ever?'

He had nothing to say. He agreed with her. How could she?

After another prolonged wait she said something he could not hear precisely. Was it 'Come closer…'? He could not credit his ears.

He made a big effort and mumbled her name. 'Come closer to me,' she said.